He should have fast-forwarded past her seductive show…

Duke's finger wavered over the forward button, urging him to do the honorable thing.

But just then Amanda's on-screen image reached for her gown's zipper. The blood pounded through his veins. The room's temperature jumped at least ten degrees. Restless tension thrummed through him. Duke dropped the remote, gladly trading his eligibility for sainthood to watch that zipper slide south.

Inch by tantalizing inch her skin revealed itself to his avid stare. In his mind's eye he inserted his hand over hers, his palm against her smooth, warm back. He could almost feel the warmth of Amanda beneath his fingers.

Finally the expanse of creamy-white flesh gave way to the shimmering silk and revealing lace of hot-pink lingerie that sent his jaw to the floor.

At that moment Duke knew he wouldn't rest until he'd personally discovered the real Amanda Matthews.

Blaze™

Dear Reader,

Amanda Matthews doesn't mean to give Duke Rawlins a private show, but when her steamy striptease video falls into the wrong man's hands, she finds herself more exposed than she bargained for!

New York detective Duke Rawlins thinks he's seen it all until Amanda Matthews blazes across his television screen in little more than a garter belt. Although Amanda swears she had no idea her boyfriend was a white-collar criminal, Duke is certain this uptown girl is hiding more than a penchant for naughty lingerie. He's determined to stay close to her until he uncovers *all* her secrets.

If you like *Silk, Lace & Videotape,* you won't want to miss my July 2002 Blaze, *In Hot Pursuit.* Duke's partner, Josh, and Amanda's best friend, Lexi, face off over a pair of handcuffs and end up *very* tied together. Visit me at www.JoanneRock.com to learn more about my future releases or to let me know what you think of my books. I'd love to hear from you!

Happy reading!

Joanne Rock

P.S. Don't forget to check out the special Blaze Web site at www.tryblaze.com.

Books by Joanne Rock

HARLEQUIN TEMPTATION
863—LEARNING CURVES

SILK, LACE & VIDEOTAPE

Joanne Rock

HARLEQUIN®

TORONTO • NEW YORK • LONDON
AMSTERDAM • PARIS • SYDNEY • HAMBURG
STOCKHOLM • ATHENS • TOKYO • MILAN • MADRID
PRAGUE • WARSAW • BUDAPEST • AUCKLAND

To wise and wonderful Catherine Mann for reading this
book while she made yet another cross-country move.
Thank you, my friend!
And to Dean,
for always helping me to live by my own light.

RECYCLED PAPER · RECYCLED PAPER

ISBN 0-373-79030-9

SILK, LACE & VIDEOTAPE

Copyright © 2002 by Joanne Rock.

This edition published by arrangement with Harlequin Books S.A.

Visit us at www.eHarlequin.com

Printed in U.S.A.

1

IN NEARLY TEN YEARS of stakeouts with the New York police force, Detective Duke Rawlins had never allowed anything to distract him from his job.

Too bad the file photo of knockout designer Amanda Matthews didn't know that.

Duke stretched in the limited space offered by his police-issued, unmarked car. He smoothed his finger over the grainy black-and-white image stapled inside his latest case file. He needed to arrest Amanda's drug-smuggling boyfriend this morning. Salivating over a Manhattan socialite with more mob connections than dinner invitations wasn't about to get the job done.

Since when had Duke started going for the mob moll type anyway? No matter how long her family had been in the social register, Amanda Matthews's father was a couturier to every mobster in the city. By the look of things, Amanda would follow right in Daddy's footsteps.

Not that it mattered to Duke.

He slapped the file closed and tossed it across the bench seat. He'd definitely been pursuing Amanda's boyfriend, Victor Gallagher, for too long.

So what if Amanda's high cheekbones and pouting lips imparted a movie-star glamour Duke found damnably attractive? She would probably stroll out of Gallagher's apartment any moment after a night of torrid sex. Maybe that little reality check would force Duke to get his mind back on his work—back on the promotion that Gallagher's conviction would solidify.

He patted his gun and the pocket that held his badge, grateful he wasn't the type of guy to get distracted on the job. Reaching for the car door handle, he prepared to face the key conviction in the Garment District's drug smuggling ring. After today, Duke would gladly banish Amanda's photo to a filing cabinet in the nether regions of the police station.

That is, if she wasn't connected to her boyfriend's crimes.

Duke started to step out into the late spring drizzle when a taxi pulled up to the apartment he'd been watching, the bright yellow cab a splash of color in a gray day. On instinct, Duke pulled his car door shut. From his angle across the street and down a few buildings, he had a view of both sides of the cab.

The newcomer was probably no one—just another artsy type who called this trendy area of the Lower West Side home.

Except that the endless feminine leg emerging from the cab didn't look like it belonged to no one.

No. This trim calf and knee was sheathed in a light veil of pink, as if some clever spider had woven a cotton candy web around that expanse of perfect flesh. Capping off the pink stocking and mouth-watering leg was a hot pink shoe that looked more suited to the bedroom than the puddle-covered pavement of West Twenty-eighth Street.

He recognized that shoe. The Barbie doll he'd bought for his niece two years ago had been wearing heels just like it. This was the first time Duke had seen such impractical footwear on a walking, talking—

Woman.

Duke swallowed hard as the second leg swung down to the concrete. A sweat broke out when a trench coat and hourglass figure slid from the cab. Light brown hair and an all-too-familiar movie-star pout made his jaw drop.

Amanda Matthews had arrived.

Duke reminded himself to breathe. To think. He had a job to do, damn it.

Unfortunately, all he could think of was how odd it seemed for Victor Gallagher's sexy girlfriend to be entering his apartment building at 9:00 a.m. rather than leaving it.

Did that thought rank as a distraction from his case, or was he thinking about it by thinking about her?

Damn.

It looked like Amanda Matthews didn't have any intention of being banished to the filing cabinet any time soon.

AMANDA HAD NEVER fully appreciated the silk lining of her trench coat until she slithered her way out of a taxi in the garment with nothing on underneath it.

Well, almost nothing.

The metal hooks on her garters scraped lightly against her thighs as she hopped a puddle on West Twenty-eighth Street. The tantalizing abrasion reminded her she did indeed wear *something* beneath the oversize camel-colored coat. But she hardly counted the pink lace merry widow and matching panties as clothes. She was prepared to bare scandalous amounts of skin for her boyfriend today if it would help shed her good-girl image. She deserved a little adventure in her life, didn't she? Before Victor could say, "let's wait until the wedding night," she would make her too-honorable beau look at her with something more than warm affection in his eyes.

Of course, Amanda had no intention of dropping her coat and praying for the best. Oh no. She'd planned today's seduction scene with the same care and precision she'd used to take her career from window dresser to fledgling designer. She wouldn't ditch the coat until she'd given her noble boyfriend a chance to view her secret weapon.

The video.

Arriving at Victor's building, Amanda patted her pocket to reassure herself the tape still rested there.

This ranked as the smartest or the dumbest thing she'd ever done.

Either way, after today she would know if she and Victor had any hope of a future together. She wasn't willing to take it on faith that physical chemistry would magically appear on her wedding night.

She reached for the door, noticing too late that her ''Passion Flower Pink'' nail polish didn't match her fuchsia ensemble as perfectly as she'd hoped. Damn. Victor was as fashion-happy as her father. What if the only thing he noticed about the scintillating striptease she'd taped for him was that her manicure clashed with her spandex and lace?

''Don't go there,'' she chided herself, refusing to allow old self-doubts to creep in now. She hadn't propelled her designs onto the runways of New York and Milan by questioning her judgment.

Before she managed to lever the heavy door open, a broad masculine hand appeared in her line of vision to do the job for her.

''Allow me,'' a silky baritone voice rumbled from behind, making her jump.

She turned to thank one of New York's nearly extinct courteous gentlemen and found herself blinking up at Sinatra blue eyes, a granite jaw complete with cleft chin, and cropped blond hair spiking in careless disarray. The stranger flashed her a gorgeous lopsided grin that packed nearly as much firepower as his multi-colored necktie emblazoned with fluorescent stars. A definite original. This man made Amanda's father's male showroom models look as bland as carbon copy Ken dolls.

Amanda forgot what she'd been about to say. The only thought in her brain was that this guy had more charisma in his pinky than those male models had in their overstuffed portfolios.

He also had a very broad chest beneath that loud necktie.

The man leaned fractionally closer, making her all too aware of the scant whisper of lace beneath her coat. His blue gaze scorched right through to her skin.

He winked. "Never a doorman around when you need one, is there?"

His words jarred her, reminding her she wasn't just daydreaming again. She was actually face-to-face with a fantasy-worthy man and she could only ogle him like an overwrought adolescent. Not that she'd spent any teenage years wearing peekaboo lace panties.

"Thank you," she managed, vaguely annoyed a handsome man could distract her from her important purpose today.

She wanted cultured, refined Victor Gallagher in her life, didn't she? She didn't need a fleeting attraction to a flashy stranger with a sinful smile.

And much too knowing eyes.

She stepped inside Victor's building and a gust of wind caught the hem of her coat. The cold breeze swirled up her trench coat and around her thighs to tickle her in shocking places. She hoped the breeze caused the ensuing tingling rush and not thoughts of the man beside her.

Amanda clutched the heavy material more tightly

to her, tormented by visions of her garters bared to the world—especially the guy standing at six o'clock.

She sensed his presence trailing slowly behind her as she rushed toward the elevator. One of the elevator doors was closing, but maybe if she hurried...

''Hold the elevator,'' she called. Picking up her pace, she was so intent on escaping the sexy man behind her, she forgot about her made-for-the-bedroom shoes and nearly twisted her ankle.

New visions arrived—even more horrible. If she took a tumble in the lobby, the man behind her would see a lot more than garters.

Stray strands of her hair were springing loose from the chic French chignon she'd struggled half an hour to create. How could a total stranger fluster her this much?

Taking long, calming breaths, Amanda waited for the next elevator and assured herself once she initiated an intimate relationship with Victor, she wouldn't feel a stray temptation like this again. She was probably just starved for male attention, considering her years of unwanted celibacy.

That had to be it.

She sure hoped so anyway because the push-up underwires her getup required were rubbing her breasts raw. Certainly that accounted for the tightening sensation in her nipples and not the slow footsteps of Blue Eyes as he approached.

She had never tried to attract much attention as a teenager because she'd been fifteen pounds overweight and relentlessly focused on succeeding in her father's glamorous world. Then later, she'd been overlooked because she was famous designer Clyde Matthews's daughter and no one wanted to risk a back seat tangle with the daughter of a man reputed to be tied to the mob.

All of which had driven her to set the fashion world on fire with her own designs—but it had also left her nearly as inexperienced as a virgin at the age of twenty-five. Her one sexual encounter with her college boyfriend in his car had resulted in the man's hasty departure to enroll in a liberal arts program somewhere in Utah. No doubt, her powerful father had influenced that decision. But Clyde Matthews hadn't objected to her relationship with his best fabric supplier, Victor Gallagher.

Maybe once she got closer to Victor, she would consider his repeated offers of marriage. All Amanda had to do was take their relationship to the next level to be sure they were really…compatible.

And try to ignore studly strangers she bumped into on the street.

Amanda stood amid the potted palm trees in the lobby, willing away a fierce attack of nerves as his footsteps grew louder, closer. Her feminine radar blinked wildly as he reached her side again. Her skin turned to gooseflesh beneath her coat. The silk lining of the trench coat teased her mercilessly.

It had to be the lingerie and spike heels making her feel this way, heightening her awareness on the most basic level. She just wasn't that type of girl. She'd gone to Catholic school, after all. She rarely went out with the party crowds of her father's fashion world. So far she'd managed to avoid the hubbub of life in the tabloids, preferring to spend her free time close to home.

And this was the *only* time in her life she hadn't worn clothing beneath her outerwear.

"Going up?" the spiky-haired stranger asked as an elevator door slid open in front of them.

That smooth voice wrought a tiny shiver. Although she didn't think gusts of wind would be a threat on an elevator, Amanda decided she couldn't be too careful at this point and hugged her coat all the tighter.

Nodding, she led the way inside the small space. Soon she would be safe inside Victor's apartment and this steamy little interlude would be over. That would be a *good* thing, right? "Tenth floor."

He pushed the button and Amanda noticed he didn't press another one for himself. Did he live on Victor's floor, too? Or was he preparing to mug her in the hallway?

She shook off her suspicion, certain criminals knew better than to wear such memorable clothing. Even if she hadn't spent her life attuning herself to fashion, she would have known that tie anywhere.

The ancient elevator lurched its way upward, causing Amanda to waver on her feet just a little. The man's hand slid under her elbow in a flash, securing her with a quick, sure grip.

He steadied her on her feet anyway. Her pulse kicked up a notch at his touch, leaving the rest of her feeling more flustered and overheated than ever.

"Maybe we should have taken the stairs," he noted, his hand falling back to his side.

"Not in these shoes." She was used to heels, but these shoes were made of little more than ribbons.

She regretted the words the moment she said them, because his blue gaze slid immediately to her feet. Then he eased up her legs, lingering on the short stretch of pale pink stocking exposed beneath the hem of her coat. Finally, he breezed over the rest of her body, his eyes meeting hers again.

The man had a lazy stare that was far too bold.

Amanda found herself wanting to show him more.

He nodded slowly. "You're right. The shoes present a problem. But that's a great coat."

Amanda stared up at the numbers flashing by as they cruised upward, certain if she met the man's searing blue eyes he would somehow guess her secret. "Thanks," she managed.

"Classy and conservative." He straightened his tie, drawing her attention back to the colorful cosmic pattern. "Right up my alley."

Amanda couldn't suppress a laugh. "I can tell."

The elevator bell chimed as they hit the tenth floor.

For a moment, Amanda forgot it was her stop. She merely soaked up the warmth emanating from this dynamic stranger, wishing she'd known more people in her life who found it so easy to laugh at themselves.

Wishing she'd known a man who could make her feel so sexy without even trying.

"Your floor?" He held the automatic doors open when they began to shut again.

She gave herself a shake. What had gotten into her? "Yes, please," she murmured, eager to escape those mesmerizing eyes.

She walked with leaden steps toward Victor's door, her enthusiasm for today's scheme significantly lessened. How could she seduce her boyfriend when a total stranger had just turned her on more in five minutes than two months' worth of kisses from Victor?

As she stood in front of apartment 10G, she considered forgetting the whole thing. After nearly overheating in the elevator, Amanda was surprised at the slight chill that tripped over her now.

Then she recalled all the time she'd spent crafting the secret weapon. She'd created the striptease video so that she could finally learn if she possessed the ability to incite a man to lust.

Not exactly the Catholic school values she'd been taught, but Amanda needed assurance he was really the right man. Besides, didn't she deserve just a *little* adventure in her life?

Shoving aside thoughts of Blue Eyes, Amanda rang Victor's doorbell.

The spiky-haired stranger materialized at her side before her summons was answered. "Hey, is Vic a friend of yours, too?"

The heated sensations came flaming back to life.

Was Blue Eyes following her? She needed to put an end to this before she did something she'd regret. Like hustle the man into a broom closet and not come out for a week or two. "Yes. We are practically engaged," she returned, pretty sure that Victor wouldn't let anyone call him "Vic."

"That's too bad." He shook his head. "I didn't realize you would be here at this early hour or I would have waited to come by."

Maybe the man did business with Victor. "It's okay. I don't usually bother Victor during his business hours, but—"

The door to apartment 10G swung open. Only the person standing there was not the man who'd practically begged Amanda to marry him.

No.

The person in Victor's apartment was an exotic dark-haired beauty with bed-rumpled hair, smeared lipstick and a man's bathrobe.

Confusion warred with shock. Surely Amanda had the wrong apartment....

Then Victor's voice shouted from the back room. "Who is it, Cindy?"

The woman in the entryway flicked her gaze over Amanda and seemed to dismiss her. She licked her lips while ogling Mr. Necktie, however.

Cindy didn't bother to greet them. She turned to shout over her shoulder. "It's for you."

Amanda's confusion turned to anger as she watched the woman's bold-as-you-please bare feet pad their way across the parquet floor to Victor's kitchen. The interloper's generous curves clearly swayed beneath the bathrobe, highlighting the woman's lack of undergarments.

Humiliation burned Amanda's eyes then singed its way through the rest of her. If not for the sudden sensation of Mr. Necktie's bracing touch at her back, she might have whipped her secret weapon across the room straight into the woman's sashaying butt.

Her elevator companion leaned close to whisper in Amanda's ear. "Maybe you should come back later." He nudged her slightly, unaware her feet were frozen to the floor.

Amanda's good-girl instincts might have won out. She might have turned and walked away from what would no doubt be an ugly scene if two-timing Victor hadn't stepped into the hallway at that moment.

"Who is it, babe—" he started before halting in his equally barefoot tracks to gape at Amanda.

How could she have ever thought she might love this man? His precisely creased pants were fastened but his belt had not yet been buckled. A silk Armani shirt fluttered at his sides, unbuttoned to reveal a sprinkling of dark chest hair and an abdomen honed to perfection at a posh gym.

How ironic that this was the most she'd ever seen of his body.

Even when he was caught in an act that revealed the blemished nature of his soul, the man had the nerve to look like an airbrushed advertisement.

His betrayal slammed through her, reminding her that no matter how successful her designs became, she'd never truly fit in her father's glamorous world. Once again, Amanda Matthews had been the outsider, only this time she hadn't even been aware of it—until now.

Her inner fury sprung to life and effectively unfroze her from her shock. That had paralyzed her. Her feet flew in Victor's direction. "You no-good, lying bastard—"

Blue Eyes slid in between her and her target. "Maybe we'd all better sit down here and sort this out." He gripped Amanda by the shoulders, his unwavering gaze fixed on her alone.

Rage burned through her, seeking any target in her path, even an undeserving one. She spewed some of that hurt anger onto Mr. Necktie.

"Who the hell are you?" Amanda's words mirrored Victor's.

Blue Eyes withdrew a small leather case from his coat pocket and flashed a shiny badge in both of their directions. His eyes remained on Amanda, however. "Detective Duke Rawlins, NYPD, at your service."

A cop?

She'd been fighting an attraction to a cop?

Amanda's anger ebbed just a little as a wave of fear took its place. In the background she heard Victor and his trollop both start talking at once, but all Amanda could think about was getting hauled off to jail. The detective had followed her into the building and right into Victor's apartment. Obviously she had more trouble on her hands than a lying, cheating boyfriend.

Had she committed some violation of the indecent exposure code? Had that gust of wind revealed more than she'd realized? What if he frisked her? Or heaven forbid, searched her? A strip search wouldn't play out well at all. She tugged her coat tie tighter.

And if she got booked as a common flasher... Amanda didn't think she'd survive the embarrassment. Her father provided more than enough Matthews family gossip for the tabloids. Her recent accolades as an up-and-coming designer in her own right would be meaningless in light of such a scandal.

Detective Rawlins pointed toward the couch. His whole demeanor had changed. The cheeky grins from the elevator had vanished. He seemed utterly at ease taking command of the room. "Ladies, I'm going to need both of you to take a seat for questioning while I take care of Mr. Gallagher."

Cindy harrumphed her way over to the couch, no longer flirting with Blue Eyes now that she knew his identity. The woman glared at Amanda, as if the morning's events were somehow *her* fault. Amanda ignored her, too worried about how she would explain jail time to her father to let Victor's other girlfriend rattle her. Amanda carefully seated herself in a wing-back chair, making sure her coat remained plastered to her thighs.

Detective Rawlins walked around the living room, his gaze seeming to absorb every detail of Victor's sparsely decorated apartment. "Vic, you're already looking at three to ten for helping your drug importer friends. If you start talking to me about your business partners, maybe I won't call the IRS about all your undeclared income."

Relief poured through Amanda as the cop read Victor his rights and arrested him on a string of charges Amanda didn't really understand. What was criminal facilitation anyway?

All she could think about was maybe she wouldn't face flasher charges now.

Amanda whispered a quick prayer of thanksgiving that she wasn't going to jail. All she had to do was keep her coat firmly cinched, answer the detective's questions, and not allow his sexy smile to unnerve her again.

Then with any luck, she could limp out of here in her fuchsia heels and go back to her safe—but respectable—existence.

2

DUKE SAVED AMANDA Matthews for last.

Not because she looked like a fifties movie star in her pink shoes and Grace Kelly hairdo. He was too professional to base his work decisions on personal lust. Besides, he knew society types were out of his league.

Instead, Duke kept Amanda waiting past noon because of her infamous last name. He thought she could be the key to important information for his case and it might help loosen her lips to let her worry a bit.

The notion teased his sex-starved senses.

Poor choice of images.

Duke looked around Victor Gallagher's apartment in an attempt to pull himself together. His thoughts—and his eyes—had strayed to the curvaceous knockout seated primly in a leather wingback chair all morning. Now, he forced himself to run through a mental checklist of police procedure to be sure every facet of the search, questioning and arrest had unfolded according to regulation.

Duke's partner had taken a rare sick day today, forcing Duke to be all the more thorough. The last thing he needed was for Gallagher to walk on some bogus technicality and blow this case for him.

Clyde Matthews's fabric supplier would be the first of many arrests in the Garment District in the next few weeks if Duke's case progressed as planned. Duke had worked for eight months gathering evidence of shady dealings in the fashion world, and starting today, he would reap the unique satisfaction of restoring justice in his backyard. Not only would he clean up the tenth precinct considerably, he would also be up for a promotion to Detective, First Grade.

Another bad guy behind bars. Another proverbial star on Duke's chest. His granddad would be proud.

Only two uniformed officers remained on the scene collecting and labeling evidence from the search. Gallagher had been carted off nearly an hour ago, and Duke had just dismissed the gold-digging tart who'd been wearing the bathrobe.

He couldn't put off questioning Amanda any longer.

She looked more vulnerable in person than in her file photo. Her fingers twisted white-knuckled around the cinched tie of her trench coat. She was obviously cold from the inside out after what had happened today.

No damn wonder.

A few hours ago she'd been ''practically'' engaged to an industry insider who looked like a walking fashion ad. Now she had a two-timing boyfriend facing at least three years in jail.

No sense feeling sorry for her. Duke knew from experience how women from her world operated. The darlings of New York's social pages could shake off a bad relationship. By noon tomorrow she'd probably be ready to have a power luncheon with her rich girlfriends to pinpoint the next ideal candidate for engagement.

Duke had been taken in by pearls and good breeding at one point in his life. He'd been left with the retreating tread marks from the designer high heels, too.

Steeling his libido for the next round with those sheer pink stockings, he approached the wingback chair. "Excuse me, Ms. Matthews?"

She started at the sound of his voice. One hand flew from her lap to her chest, as if to still her heart. Or perhaps to clutch that damn coat more tightly to her neck. What on earth was she wearing under that trench coat anyway?

As if in answer to his question, the bunched coat fabric on her thighs slid slightly open, revealing two more inches of stocking and no sign of a skirt hem.

For one riveting moment, Duke thought he spied the top of a stocking. His body stirred in wholly inappropriate ways, even after she secured the folds of the trench coat in her lap again.

Damn. Just how short was her skirt?

"Yes?" She looked up at him with wary hope in her dark brown eyes. "May I go now?"

"I'm afraid not. I need to ask you a few questions

about your relationship with Victor Gallagher.'' Of course, any information she wanted to volunteer about Gallagher's business or her father's mob connections would be helpful, he thought, taking a seat on the couch across from her.

''He's in serious trouble?'' Concern knitted her brows.

''Felony charges with a penalty of three to ten. I'd call it serious.'' Did she really care after discovering him in such a compromising situation? The notion bugged Duke. Amanda had a gentle air about her, despite the killer outfit she must be wearing under that trench coat. She seemed too refined to be connected to a criminal like Gallagher. Despite his gangster reputation, her infamous father had obviously sheltered his only daughter.

She rubbed her upper arms as if to ward off a chill. ''What exactly did he do?''

''A number of things. He's been helping to import drugs into the States, using his fabric business as a cover.'' He tried to keep the explanation simple, not wanting to dissuade Amanda from cooperating. What if she still carried a torch for the guy?

She looked surprised. And frightened.

''I had no idea.'' She worried the fullness of her lower lip with straight, white teeth. ''He seemed so...cultured. He doesn't seem like a street thug.''

Duke wondered if she knew the extent of her father's business dealings. He'd be willing to bet the elder Matthews didn't seem like a street thug, either, but he rubbed elbows with the oldest—and toughest—gang in the city. "You're a window dresser, Ms. Matthews?"

"I create windows for my father, but I've started my own design business as well," she corrected him, then smiled. "I make the distinction so my father doesn't slip back into thinking I'm his personal maid and secretary. How did you know what I do?"

"You're a line item in Gallagher's file. I only checked into the basics though." Her ritzy address, her perfect education, her relationship with Victor— which had seemed fairly superficial from the reports Duke had received. Now that Duke had met Amanda, he couldn't imagine why Gallagher wouldn't have claimed her already. The guy had made a colossal mistake as far as Duke could see.

"You were planning to arrest him from the moment I first saw you this morning, weren't you?"

Duke thought it wise not to reveal the exact nature of his thoughts when he'd first seen her this morning. Purely carnal. "Sorry I couldn't have spared you the inconvenience, but—"

"It's Amanda. Please." She smiled at him in a way that managed to be both warm and distant. She apparently couldn't shake her boarding school manners even in the event of police questioning, no matter how much the proceedings disrupted her day—her life.

Duke would have preferred to maintain as many social barriers between them as he possibly could— especially with his mind straying back to that tantalizing glimpse of stocking every other minute. He wasn't about to be rude, however. "Amanda." The name pleased him as it rolled off his tongue. "Could you tell me why you were visiting Victor Gallagher today?"

She blanched. She shifted uncomfortably in her seat. She might as well have shouted through a megaphone that she was about lie to him. "It was just a simple...social call."

Duke hadn't suspected Clyde Matthews's daughter of anything save poor judgment in boyfriends, but now he began to wonder. She looked as guilty as a sinner on Sunday. "Apparently you were going to surprise him...?"

She adjusted the coat over her lap for the tenth time. "What makes you say that?"

"If he knew you were on your way over, don't you think he would have showed his lady friend to the door?"

Her cheeks grew as pink as her stockings. "Then it's a good thing I didn't tell him I was on my way, isn't it? I never would have known."

God knew he could relate to how she felt. He'd learned quickly that the cop groupies he'd dated when he first arrived in New York weren't picky about which detective they slept with. Duke's attempts to be selective since then had left him with long dry spells. In fact, his current dry spell had him drooling over Amanda Matthews's trim calves beneath those sheer stockings, and wreaking havoc on his concentration.

Duke squelched his sympathy, needing to focus on his job. "So your visit today was social?"

She nodded, looking a bit calmer now.

Duke moved on, filing away her reactions along with her answers. He would uncover Amanda's secrets sooner or later, even if he had to keep her and her very short skirt here for another hour.

Heaven help him.

He withdrew a pen and paper to give himself something to do, a way to distract himself. "And how would you characterize your relationship overall? Is it mostly social, or do the two of you discuss business when you spend time together?"

Amanda heard the detective's question, but she didn't want to answer it. She watched his pen seesaw back and forth over his thumb, mesmerized, and tried to think of a way around the question. She didn't need another cop nosing into her family's business. Her father might look like a favored son of the mob, but he only made suits for them. The association had troubled her for years, but she had yet to talk her father out of his bigwig clients.

"Victor and I rarely discussed business," she replied, shifting her position in the gray leather wingback chair.

Her limbs were stiff with the tension of her rigid posture, but she refused to unveil another millimeter of stocking. Had it been her imagination, or had Duke

Rawlins's eyes widened at the revelation of so much thigh a few moments ago?

Had he been admiring her stockings or contemplating indecent exposure charges?

"When you did discuss business, what sorts of things would come up?"

"Victor is not on the creative side of my business, so there wasn't really much for us to discuss. He'd encourage me to find out what kinds of fabric I thought my father might want for his next collection ahead of time so that Victor could be first in line to give him good prices on it."

The pen stopped seesawing. "Did you?"

His intent look made her wonder if she should have called a lawyer. But then, what did she have to hide?

Besides the obvious.

"Would it be a crime if I did?" She would brazen this out.

"No, Amanda."

Why had she asked him to call her that? Her name on his lips had a way of slithering over her like a slow caress. As if in response, the ties on her merry widow began to unravel from their loose knot, threatening to leave Amanda as unbound and jiggling as that hussy Victor had been sleeping with. She sucked in her belly, hoping to ease off any extra pressure from the garment.

This particular article of clothing was not designed to wear for more than five minutes anyway. It was intended to drive a man wild in thirty seconds flat.

No wonder she was springing out of it. "Well, I have never been able to anticipate my father's creative direction, so I never supplied Victor with any inside information. He found out what Clyde Matthews wanted when the rest of us did."

Her father thrived on the aesthetic of a successful artist—the lunches in trendy cafés, the shows in Paris and Milan, the endless parade of up-and-coming designers, artists and models that peopled his studio at all hours. It didn't seem to bother him that his artistic immersion had never left time in his life for anything else, including his only child.

Duke Rawlins cleared his throat and set aside his hyperactive pen. "So how long have you known Gallagher?"

Something in his demeanor, the way he leaned forward slightly, made the question sound personal.

The silk lining of her coat teased the tops of her breasts with every breath she took. The fabric would be teasing a whole lot more if her merry widow sprung loose and wound up around her ankles. "For almost a year."

And Victor had never given her more than a goodnight kiss in all that time. Obviously, he'd had a more pleasing partner to fulfill his other needs.

The dog.

"Has he ever offered you illegal drugs?"

"I beg your pardon?" Righteous indignation fired through her.

"You know, methamphetamines, crack, ecstasy, any number of lab-created specialties—"

"He most certainly did not!" Just who did Duke Rawlins think she was? Amanda might not be wearing anything but lace and satin beneath her coat, but she was not *that* kind of girl.

Trying to coerce her boyfriend into an intimate relationship ranked as her biggest moral transgression to date.

"I have to ask, Amanda." At least the detective had the decency to flash her a semi-apologetic smile. "If it makes you feel any better, you don't seem to fit my profile of a drug user anyway."

Before Amanda could splutter a retort, a uniformed police officer approached.

"Excuse me, Detective." The young woman lifted a shopping bag to show Duke Rawlins. "We are finished here. I checked and rechecked all the labels and the evidence-gathering procedures. We dug up a few bills of sale for fabric, a list that might be potential drug buyers. Everything is in order."

Amanda eyed the tall female officer labeled R. Patterson as the woman spoke with Amanda's interrogator. Ms. Patterson didn't look like the type to ever wind up half-naked in a police interrogation. Amanda would also lay odds that R. Patterson would kick her boyfriend's butt if he dared to treat *her* the way Victor had treated Amanda.

Amanda had that kind of confidence in her professional world, but on a personal level, she couldn't seem to get her act together. She'd let her father take advantage of her half her life, and now she'd obviously allowed Victor to do the same thing.

"Thanks, Patterson," Duke Rawlins called over his shoulder as the woman left with the last remaining uniformed officer.

Leaving Amanda alone with a very sexy detective.

The quiet of Victor's apartment seemed to intensify after the door shut behind the departing officers. Amanda became aware of the clock ticking on the wall, the hum of the overhead light in the kitchen.

And she became keenly aware of Duke Rawlins's intensely blue eyes upon her.

How could she feel such tangible lust for a man she'd just met? A man who'd arrested her boyfriend, witnessed the biggest humiliation of her life and held her captive with his interrogation while an even bigger humiliation threatened in the form of a renegade merry widow.

What a disaster.

"I guess that's it, Amanda." Detective Rawlins tucked his notepad inside his leather jacket pocket, but made no move to stand. "Would you do me a favor?"

For a moment, she lost herself in the depths of his blue eyes. The color matched the fluorescent blue on several of his necktie stars.

She found herself saying, "I will if I can."

His crooked grin sent a thrill through her, far more potent than the silk lining on her bare skin. "Call me if you think of anything else about your boyfriend that might help me.''

She took his card and read over it absently. "He's not my boyfriend anymore, Detective," she clarified.

Amanda sensed the heat of a blush start on her neck and spread to her cheeks. Why had she felt the need to tell him that?

"Can't say I blame you after today," he returned, slowly rising to his feet. "And please, call me Duke."

Amanda scrambled to follow him, ready to flee the apartment and those intense eyes as fast as possible.

Too late she remembered her merry widow.

It slid about two inches south, the bra cups rolling like window shades under the curve of each breast. Amanda would give anything to untie and retie her entire ensemble before she walked out the door, but not while the tempting detective remained in the apartment with her.

She folded her arms over her chest. "Thank you, Duke."

The words sounded throaty and breathless and very flirtatious when in fact, fear for her costume merely edged Amanda a bit closer to hyperventilating.

She inched toward the door, praying she could escape without flashing Duke. Even her shoes were coming untied, but she refused to bend over to secure them.

"Well, if that's all then...?" she prodded, waiting only for his official nod so she could slink back home after her horrid day.

He scrubbed a hand along his square jaw and frowned. "Actually, would you mind stopping by the precinct tomorrow to answer a few more questions? Say around eleven?"

"More questions?" Not that she was in a position to argue, but what more could she tell him about Victor? Apparently she hadn't known him at all.

Besides, she'd have to face the allure of that chiseled jaw and sinful smile all over again.

"I always think of a few more things after the case settles in my mind for a day." He shrugged as if in apology. "I could send a car over to your father's studio if it would help."

"That's not necessary." Now there was an image—New York's Finest descending on Clyde Matthews's showroom. What if some bigwig crime boss had scheduled a fitting with her father or something? Social awkwardness at its height. Besides, Amanda wasn't sure how she would explain her run-in with the police to her father in the first place. "I'll drop by at eleven."

Once she put some clothes on, conversing with Duke wouldn't be nearly as...provocative.

She hoped.

"Great." He strode toward the door and opened it for her. "I'll see you then."

Freedom beckoned. Escape loomed so near.

Yet Duke halted her before she could take step into the hallway. "You'll twist an ankle in that shoe unless you tie it.'' He allowed the door to swing closed as his gaze lingered on her foot.

The pink ribbons meant to tie her foot into the shoe had completely unraveled. As with her merry widow, Amanda hadn't double knotted any portion of her outfit. Now if she bent over to adjust her shoe, her merry widow was history.

If she left her pink high heel untied, she'd hobble right out of it before she reached the elevator.

An untied shoe seemed like a little thing in comparison to finding out her boyfriend had been cheating on her, that her judgment in men led her into a relationship with a criminal.

But it threatened to be more than she could bear in light of everything else. She bit one ''Passion Flower Pink'' nail and tried to decide what to do next.

She suspected the moment had turned awkward when Duke's brows lifted in unison.

He jabbed a thumb in the general direction of her foot. ''Want me to tie it for you?''

A flood of gratitude had her head bobbing agreement and her mind making mental notes to buy a whole table full of tickets for the Policemen's Ball this year. ''Would you mind?''

He didn't move for a long moment. Perhaps he was surprised she'd taken him up on his offer.

She wanted to offer an excuse for her odd behavior—perhaps that she'd been afflicted with a debilitating spine condition that inhibited her mobility. Or that she'd sprained her index finger last week and she found it difficult to manage the ties.

But she'd never been any good at lying.

Finally, he reached for her arms. Amanda might have stepped back, but she would have stepped out of her shoe. Or out of her merry widow.

"Why don't you have a seat for just a minute?" he prompted, guiding her to the arm of the wingback.

She nodded like a complacent five-year-old, having her shoe tied before running out to the bus. Only Duke's touch didn't make her feel a bit like a five-year-old.

He kneeled at her feet, anchoring her shoe with his thigh and gently steering her foot into position on the sole. For a moment, his thumb and forefinger ringed her ankle, imprisoning her leg and putting her senses on alert. Then his broad hands glided over the silky finish of her stockings, the rough pads of his thumbs catching the material ever so slightly to send shocks of pleasure up her calf, to her thigh, and beyond....

Her eyes fluttered closed at the unaccustomed sensation. What a shock *he* would get if he followed that trail with his hands.

In an instant, his hands turned brusque and professional again, tying her shoe with a firm tug on both ends of the knot.

She opened her eyes to find him staring up at her, his gaze broadcasting even more heat than his hands. She made a small sound—a little hiss of breath like a kettle releasing excess steam.

He practically jumped up from the floor. "Are you going to be okay?" His voice scratched along her nerves, low and gruff.

She nodded, remembering her haste to make an exit. "Yes. I am...um...sorry."

"You've had a hell of a day." He extended his hand as if to shake hers.

Amanda accepted it, regretting those few seconds where she would only have one hand to secure the trench coat. "Thank you, Duke."

Their palms clasped briefly, though Duke snatched his hand back almost as quickly as she did. With her father's reputation as a friend of the mob, she'd grown used to men running from her. Still, she couldn't help but think Duke's retreat didn't have anything to do with fear of being a mob target.

"I'll see you tomorrow," he reminded her.

If Amanda hadn't just been unceremoniously dumped by her boyfriend today, she might have actually looked forward to seeing Duke again. God knew she was attracted. Too attracted. Maybe that was part of the problem.

Her judgment in men was more faulty than San Andreas if today's fiasco was any indication. She wasn't about to get burned by a flashy police detective who seemed to know where her on switch was located.

"Bye." Amanda tossed the word over her shoulder as she left the apartment. She trotted to the elevator as fast as her pink heels would allow her. In less than sixty seconds, she was out the door and in a cab headed back uptown, safe from Duke's knowing eyes and tempting grin.

Only then did Amanda allow herself to relax. The cabdriver was too busy swearing at traffic and the participants on his talk radio program to notice her furtive attempts to retie her merry widow, shielding her chest with her lapels.

She could hardly believe she'd escaped Victor's apartment without anyone noticing she wore next to nothing beneath her coat. Relief slowly drifted over her, easing the aching muscles in a body that had been rigid for too many hours.

She'd made it out with her dignity and her secret weapon in tact. Amanda patted her coat pocket to reassure herself it still rested there.

She found nothing.

Ohmigod. Horrified, she patted her other pocket.

Nothing.

The cabdriver's swearing faded to the background as panic seized her. The traffic lights and midday pedestrians blurred outside the windows, her whole attention focused on searching the taxicab seats in the hope her tape had fallen out of her pocket since she'd hopped into the car.

No luck.

She'd lost her secret weapon.

3

DUKE LINGERED IN the doorframe after Amanda left Gallagher's apartment. He'd watched her click her way to the elevator in those hot pink Barbie doll heels, her walk as confident as if she'd been in running shoes. Behind him, the room already seemed too quiet, less animated.

Damn.

He'd let her breathy voice and glimpses of stocking distract him from his questioning—something that hadn't happened in nearly ten years on the job with the NYPD. He'd covered his butt by asking her to stop by the precinct tomorrow, knowing the surroundings would keep his mind focused on his case and not Amanda's legs.

Still, he hoped like hell she wore pants.

The ringing of his cell phone provided a welcome interruption.

He flipped open the speaker as he stalked Gallagher's apartment one last time. "Rawlins."

The male voice on the other end didn't bother with salutations. "The word at the station is that Amanda Matthews looks even better in person than in her file photo."

Duke's laid-up partner, Josh Winger, had obviously heard the scoop on the day's arrest already. "Hey, Winger. If you weren't such a wuss you could have seen her for yourself."

"A few more hours and the doc swears I'm non-contagious. Want me to come in and go over the evidence with you?"

Josh had three more years on the force than Duke, but the two of them had been teamed up more often than not since Duke joined the NYPD. They did a solid rendition of good cop/bad cop, and their investigative styles complemented each other.

But Duke hadn't minded going solo today. Josh would have given him hell if he had seen how Amanda had rattled him.

"I've got it covered." Duke glanced through Gallagher's CD collection, looking for any stone left unturned in the earlier search. Maybe he'd find that final piece of damning evidence—some irrefutable link between Victor and his drug buddies. "Why don't you watch a few more *Starsky and Hutch* reruns and see if you can pick up a couple of pointers."

"The only thing I'm learning from *Starsky and Hutch* is that we're getting rooked on our standard-issue vehicle. I'm thinking we need to talk to the deputy inspector about issuing us something cooler, something packing a little more horsepower."

Finding nothing in the CDs, Duke moved to the bookshelf, another area that sometimes went overlooked in a search. He found it odd that the small collection lacked a single title on fashion or fabric. "You get the shakes driving over fifty-five anyway. My granddaddy always used to say 'don't bite off more than you can chew.'"

"To hear you tell it, Duke, your granddaddy spoke in pithy wisdom from the moment you were born. Did you just make up this ancestor so you could spout clichés and old wives' tales?"

"My granddad would kick your city slicker ass if he knew you implied he was an old wife." Duke smiled to think about it. Granddad had a deep suspicion of New York City, but he'd applauded Duke's decision to police the Big Apple, assuring him there wasn't a city in the world that needed a Rawlins so badly. "Besides, aren't you grateful he made sure I always have something to say?"

Josh groaned. "Now I know who to blame. Call me if you find anything more over there, you hear me? I don't want you blowing your promotion because you didn't have me to help you out."

"Go pop your pills, old man. I've got it covered." Duke flipped the receiver closed before Josh could quibble.

He would make Detective, First Grade, without any help from his partner. Josh had made the upward move last year, and Duke's review approached at the end of May. Once Duke cleaned up the Garment District with a round of solid felony arrests this spring, his record would be prime for an upgrade.

So shall you scale the stars...another bit of Granddad's wisdom. Maybe a promotion in the police department wasn't quite so poetic, but Duke worked with what he had. He loved this job.

He headed to the couch cushions, often a goldmine for scraps of notepaper or maybe an incriminating bill of some sort. Gallagher's couch looked like it benefited from frequent maid service, however.

He moved to the wingback next. The chair still held a trace of Amanda Matthews's scent—something clean and rain-washed and simple. Like one flower instead of ten.

She was a mix of contradictions. The conservative trench coat and straightforward fragrance seemed at odds with her starlet hairstyle and pink stockings. Any way Duke added it up, Amanda still emerged from the equation appealing as hell.

Too bad she was a society fixture and mixed up with a criminal to boot. No matter how good she smelled, Amanda Matthews earned a place on Duke's personal "off-limits" list.

Heaven knew, he could spend hours debating Ms. Matthews's charms, but he had a job to finish. Duke ordered his nose to ignore the flowery temptations as he lifted the gray leather cushion.

A black rectangular case slid to the floor.

"What the..." How had the search team missed this earlier today? Duke rolled on a pair of latex gloves and bent to retrieve the item.

He opened the case, confirming his suspicion that

a videotape rested inside. A white sticker labeled it "Private" in pencil.

Storing the evidence in a plastic bag, Duke pondered the handwriting on the sticker. He might not have a graphology degree, but he sensed a deliberateness in the dark stroke of the lines as if the writer had really meant the "Private" warning.

The thrill of crime busting snaked through him—the same thirst for justice that had pushed him through four years of college and almost a decade on the force. He couldn't wait to go review the tape tonight at the precinct.

It took him less than an hour to make a final sweep of the place and talk to the building superintendent about Gallagher's comings and goings. Duke made a few last notes and then headed for the lobby, hoping to get back to the station before commuter traffic kicked in.

He was ducking under the potted palms near the elevators when a snappy click of high heels grabbed his attention.

Amanda Matthews had returned.

So did Duke's response to her. He'd been hoping his earlier lust had been a fluke, but his current physical affliction assured him he wanted her.

Duke took advantage of her distracted state to study her. She'd obviously gone home and changed. Her trench coat flung wide open now, revealing a black turtleneck sweater he'd be willing to bet was cashmere. Gray wool trousers covered every inch of her luscious legs and black leather boots encased her feet, their heels as high as the Barbie doll shoes had been. Her light brown hair remained in the high-class twist at the back of her head, although more strands fell forward now to frame her face. A small leather satchel swung on her arm in time with her fast steps.

She looked like a confident fashion executive now, whereas earlier, she'd seemed nervous and shy. All of which had Duke wondering what the hell she was up to.

Struggling to put his duty as a law enforcement official ahead of his hunger for a small taste of Amanda's smooth skin, Duke strode closer. "Amanda?"

The word halted her, dragging her attention from the elevator doors toward him. The satchel she carried swayed like a pendulum for a moment, then slowed to a stop along with her.

Now that he had a better view of her face, he could tell she wasn't as confident as her posture suggested. Little lines of worry creased her brow and set her full lips in a straight slash.

She seemed to take a minute to compose herself. Clearly, she hadn't thought she would be seeing him here. "Detective."

With a great deal of effort, he managed to flash his charming grin, his good cop facade. "Call me Duke."

Her answering smile seemed forced, a difficult unveiling of her teeth rather than an act to light up her delicate face.

Damn. He really did not want to discover Amanda was party to her boyfriend's criminal activities. Why did she have to look so guilty?

"Right. Duke."

When she didn't offer any explanation for her presence, Duke prodded her. "Returning to the scene of the crime?"

Amanda struggled to formulate an answer. She hadn't expected him to be here an hour after he'd finished questioning her. She had hoped to talk the superintendent or maybe a maid into letting her inside Victor's apartment.

"Believe me, I didn't want to return to this building." That much was true. Memories of discovering Victor's infidelity only reminded her of her inability to interest a man in a real relationship. She'd lost fifteen pounds and spent two years figuring out how to make herself look as attractive as one of her showroom windows, and still no luck. She'd nursed the hope that the secret weapon would somehow help her get her personal life on track before the whirlwind of the fall fashion shows, before her chaotic professional life took over again. But now she'd lost the tape before she'd ever had the chance to try it out.

Not that she would have wanted to after what happened with her ex-boyfriend this morning.

When Duke only waited, smiling politely and blocking her path with his broad shoulders and six-foot frame, Amanda explained, "I thought I lost

something at Victor's this morning." No harm in revealing that, right?

Duke frowned. "I went over it again after you left
and didn't find a wallet or keys or anything. The place
is clean."

Should she tell him it wasn't a wallet? Maybe he
had found her tape and mistaken it for Victor's.

No. She wouldn't risk having to explain herself to
him, because she sure as heck couldn't lie to a cop—
not after all those years in Catholic school. Maybe
she'd dropped the tape on the street. She prayed a
yellow cab had already run over it.

And if a stranger on the street picked up the tape,
at least they wouldn't know who she was. She supposed there was a certain comfort in anonymity.

"Oh. Maybe I'll just look around the elevators and
the hallways." She waited for him to move out of her
way, but his fluorescent stars and spiky hair remained
firmly in her line of vision.

"I'll give you a hand. What did you say you lost?"
He finally stepped back to clear her path, but his body
shadowed hers on one side.

His proximity sang along her nerves and caused her
skin to tingle. Apparently her earlier attraction to
Duke hadn't been related to her slinky lingerie or her
bubble gum shoes. She'd swathed herself in cashmere
and leather after spending six hours in nothing but
lace, yet she could still feel the heat of his body right
through her heavy clothes.

"Umm...my date book." She found herself lying

in spite of herself. She had all she could do to string words together around this man, let alone keep her secret weapon a secret. "It wasn't really important anyway."

He gave her a reproving stare, the kind that would have had her biting her nails this morning. But now that she had her clothes on she didn't feel quite so intimidated by this man. Mostly she just felt...turned on.

"It must have been important to drag you all the way back here."

She shook her head, relaxing a bit now that it seemed Duke hadn't discovered her videotape. She had probably dropped it on the street as she was getting into the cab anyway. "Not as important as I thought. Maybe I did just need to revisit the scene of the crime to sort of process the day."

Duke studied her, scrubbing his hand over a five o'clock shadow. "What a jerk, huh?" he finally said, as if he'd decided it was okay to talk to her man-to-woman instead of maintaining his detective role. He jammed his fists in the pockets of his pants.

Amanda smiled to think the man might have won out. She'd been curious about—okay, majorly attracted to—Duke from the moment she'd first seen him. "No kidding. Thank God I found out before things got any more serious." Her cheeks grew hot as she heard herself speak the words. "That is, before we talked anymore about marriage."

"You were really thinking of marrying that guy?"

Duke lowered his voice on the last few words as an older couple strode by them with three yapping lap-dogs on their way to the elevator.

Amanda could hardly believe it herself, given what she'd learned about him today. How could she have been so blind about Victor? She'd been so focused on launching her first year of designs, so fixated on succeeding professionally, that she hadn't paid much attention to her personal relationships.

She shrugged. "We seemed to have a lot in com-mon—our business, our social circles—"

Duke laughed. His eyes darkened and his gaze nar-rowed. "You only need one thing in common for a marriage, Amanda, and those aren't it."

Intrigued, she leaned a bit closer. Was it really the words or the man that drew her? "And what's that?"

Before he could respond, a group of schoolkids drifted in the front doors.

Duke grabbed her hand and pulled her out of the flow of elevator traffic. He seemed to scout the back of the lobby and, finding it acceptable, he tugged her into a quiet corner by an antiquated snack machine. "All you need is chemistry. I thought everybody knew that."

Amanda wondered if he realized he still held her hand. The warmth of his palm engulfed her fingers. An innocent touch?

Not on the receiving end. Amanda was rapidly overheating at that small intimacy combined with the nearness of his broad chest, a unique effect of this man.

"I don't know...." If Duke's preposterous statement about chemistry was true, Amanda had more reason to marry a stranger like Duke Rawlins than Victor. "I think you need to base a relationship on more than that."

Duke shook his head, his blue eyes never leaving hers. "Not me. When I find the right chemistry, I'm not going to waste time comparing interests, political parties or astrological signs, I'm just going to jump in with both feet."

Was it her imagination, or did he look as bemused by this attraction as she felt?

"Really?" Amanda wished she could be that daring. She'd been overprotected most of her life. Only in the last few years had she risked her father's disapproval by undertaking her own design projects and seeking out an intimate relationship. Although the former had been wonderfully successful, the latter had left her feeling a little wary. Still, she couldn't squelch the hunger for adventure that had gnawed at her from the moment she'd slipped into her merry widow this morning.

A hunger which Duke's presence currently fed and stirred at the same time.

"What if you pick the wrong person?" She knew she couldn't bounce back from something like that.

Duke rubbed his thumb across the center of her palm and pressed the hollow in her hand, a gesture which provoked unnerving repercussions throughout the rest of her body.

"Wouldn't be the first time." The stern expression that crossed his face told her he didn't relish the thought of making a big mistake.

Yet he didn't move away, didn't pull back.

In fact, he loomed within tantalizing reach. Did she drift closer or did he? Caught up in his "live for the moment" attitude, Amanda allowed herself to be mesmerized by his eyes.

"I don't know if I could ever take risks like that." She whispered the words more to herself than to him.

Her blood pounded out the beat of her heart in the palm of her hand where he touched her. The rhythm joined them somehow, connected them in an elemental way.

"I think we should find out," he whispered back, so close she couldn't think of anything else.

Her attention shifted to his mouth, which seemed to be on a collision course with her own. A moment before contact, her eyes drifted shut in anticipation.

She did not bother to deny him. Her lips seemed to part on their own, welcoming the hot stroke of his tongue, the pressure of his mouth on hers.

The electronic hum of the snack machine faded along with the shuffle of people on the other side of the elevators. Their quiet corner closed in around them, the space igniting with the heat they generated.

Duke wrapped his hands around her waist, then slid

them up her spine, urging her closer into the hard wall of his chest.

The silk lining of her trench coat might have teased her earlier today, when Duke had been within a few feet of her nearly naked body. But the sensation paled in comparison to the caress of cashmere now that his heated body pressed insistently against the other side.

Duke breathed in the clean scent of her, so hot for her soft curves and welcoming mouth that he couldn't think straight. Blood roared in his ears, deafening him to everything but Amanda's shallow breaths, her tiny sighs as he moved his hands over her hips.

He'd been looking for an excuse to kiss her, thinking if he could only have one taste, he'd satisfy his curiosity and get her out of his head. Now he knew that one taste would tease him forever until he had more.

Much more.

The leather satchel she'd been carrying slid to the floor with a thunk—snapping his attention away from Amanda for a split second just as he'd started to pull her hips to his. In broad daylight. In the lobby of an apartment building. What the hell was the matter with him?

"Amanda." He held himself still, unable to remove his hands from her just yet. He knew better than this. She was a princess in New York's fashion society. He was a damn frog in a small pond and he had no desire to enter her glitzy world. Especially not when she could be a suspect in his current case.

Still, it soothed his ego to see her slow return to reality. Her lips remained parted for a long moment, her cheeks flushed and her hair slipping from its twist. Duke mentally placed her in his bed, imagining just how she would look if he'd been making love to her with more than his mouth.

"Amanda." The word sounded harsh, his voice rough with sexual frustration.

Her eyes flew open, her flush growing deeper.

"Sorry," she murmured, as if that particular remark fell frequently from her lips. She focused on retrieving her satchel from the floor, her hands a sudden flurry of awkward movement.

Damn.

He stepped back, prying his fingers from her body, afraid he would kiss her all over again in some misguided attempt to apologize. "Don't be." He pulled her to her feet again, unwilling to let her walk away looking so bereft. "You kiss like an angel."

Or like a temptress from a teenage fantasy.

But Amanda Matthews seemed like the kind of woman who would appreciate the first analogy more.

She adjusted the leather strap on her shoulder and rewarded him with a tentative smile. "Really?"

Duke stifled a groan. Just how innocent was she? Maybe Victor Gallagher had taken a lover because his girlfriend, the mobster's daughter, was off-limits until her wedding night. The idea made sense, considering Amanda had been going into Victor's apartment building this morning rather than leaving it.

No matter that she'd probably been wearing a killer skirt and real, honest-to-goodness stockings underneath her conservative trench coat. She had an inherent modesty about her, an old-fashioned sense of grace and propriety she broadcasted in everything from her fifties starlet hairdo to her perfect posture.

He squeezed her hand and nodded, knowing he was already in way over his head. "Really. I didn't mean to get so...carried away."

She flashed him a high-wattage smile—definitely the fantasy temptress variety—and made him rethink his ideas about her all over again. "You won't hear me complaining."

It would have been so easy to kiss her again. Amanda obviously wouldn't mind. He wanted to touch her so badly his muscles twitched with the effort to restrain himself. But Duke forced himself to think about the consequences.

Despite what he'd spouted about chemistry and jumping in with both feet, Duke knew he'd have to give some thought to involving himself with Amanda Matthews. How wise would it be for a New York detective to lose his head with a sheltered daughter of a possible mobster? A sheltered daughter who'd been lying through her teeth when she'd said she returned to Victor's building for her date book.

Maybe she was just having a hard rebound after her bout with her indiscreet boyfriend this morning. Surely that accounted for the impassioned kiss more than anything.

Duke nodded toward the lobby. "I've got to get back to the precinct and go over today's evidence. You need a ride downtown?" He asked even though he knew better than to spend too much time in her tempting presence. His granddad would kick his butt if he left a woman stranded.

She shook her head, effectively freeing a few more strands of hair from the slipping knot at the back of her head. Duke's fingers itched to pull the pins from the caramel-colored mass and see it fall down around her shoulders.

"I've got to get back to the showroom to work on a window for my father. You still want me to stop by the station tomorrow?"

"I'd appreciate it." They reached the lobby doors and he pushed one side open for her, remembering how they'd met just that morning.

The sexy look she sent sizzling his way told him she was remembering, too. "See you at eleven."

She clicked her way down the street, her trench coat waving a sassy goodbye as it moved in time with her confident step. She had a walk to turn heads, stop traffic and make Duke forget what the hell he was doing.

He'd held the door of Gallagher's apartment building for at least five people by the time she turned the corner at Twenty-eighth Street, out of his sight.

He knew she'd be very much on his mind, however, when he went to the station to review the day's evidence for his case against Gallagher.

Her kisses had been hot as a siren's, but her reaction afterward smacked of an innocence that warned him to exercise caution. Amanda Matthews's mobster father didn't intimidate him one bit, but her old-fashioned values and conservative approach gave him pause.

He would proceed very slowly with her, starting tomorrow when she stopped by the precinct at eleven.

Until then, he needed to get his head back into his case and review all the findings of his investigative team today.

And he planned to start by finding out what was on that videotape.

4

AMANDA FUMBLED WITH her keys outside her apartment door. Her overprotective father had insisted she install three different locks to secure the loft that served as her workroom and her home. Normally, she didn't mind the extra time required to unlock each one, but now that Duke Rawlins's kiss hummed in her veins, her key ring jumped out of her hands twice before her door was tugged open from the inside.

Her best friend, Lexi Mansfield, stood inside the loft, her black toy poodle at her feet. Lexi had her own apartment on Columbus Circle, but she stopped by Amanda's often enough to have a closet full of clothes stashed in the hallway. No doubt Lexi had sought out Amanda to hear how the secret weapon had gone over with Victor. Garbed in thigh-high leather boots, a skirt printed with a snakeskin design and a big black angora sweater, the petite brunette possessed an outrageous style that often masked her status as one of New York's most celebrated fashion reviewers.

Ignoring the jumping and yapping of her little dog, Lexi clucked her tongue and frowned. "You're giving Muffin a nervous breakdown with all that rattling around out there, girlfriend.'' She clutched Amanda's arm with perfectly manicured red talons and pulled her friend inside. ''Come on in here. You look like you need a drink.''

Amanda nodded numbly, not sure whether she was relieved to see Lexi or not. On her short walk home, Amanda had convinced herself the wisest course of action would be to fall into bed and forget the day— the kiss—ever happened. ''I'll have water,'' she murmured as she listened to Lexi click her way across the hardwood floors to the small kitchen, the sound echoed by Muffin's nails tapping along behind her.

Lexi had been Amanda's best friend since they'd roomed together at boarding school. They shared an interest in clothes that went all the way back to the time Amanda had created a spandex micro-mini dress complete with matching headband for Lexi's Malibu Barbie doll in second grade.

While Amanda sank into her leather couch, Lexi returned with a cup of hot tea and two gingersnaps perched on the saucer. Even as a part-time resident of Amanda's apartment, Lexi knew her way around the kitchen far better than Amanda ever had. ''Have a cookie, you'll feel better. I didn't know what else to do while I was waiting for you, so I baked cookies.''

Great. Just the sort of temptation that would put ten pounds back on her hips in a blink. Still, Amanda smiled at the way her friend blatantly ignored her request for water. The tea tasted better anyway, and it quieted her nerves just a little. At least she felt soothed until she closed her eyes and saw Duke's startling blue gaze emblazoned inside her eyelids.

Her cup and saucer clattered in her hands. Swiping aside a stack of fabric swatches she'd been working with the day before, Amanda set the teacup on an oversize trunk that served as her coffee table. "Thank you."

Lexi perched on a tall director's chair across from her, Muffin curling at her feet. "The curiosity is choking me over here. How did it go?" She looked Amanda up and down. "And please tell me you knew better than to wear all that wool to seduce a man, didn't you?"

Amanda snorted. "I knew better."

Lexi leaped out of her chair and plummeted onto the sofa beside Amanda. Her cloud of long black hair floated behind her, kept in motion by Lexi's natural restless energy. Muffin ran in circles, catching the air of excitement. "It worked, didn't it? I knew you looked different somehow. Your eyes are sort of starry or something."

Amanda stifled a groan as she thought of the fluorescent pattern on Duke Rawlins's tie. "They are definitely *not* starry. And thankfully, the plan blew up in my face."

Briefly, she outlined her horrendous day from the moment she'd walked into Victor's apartment alongside a cop, to her realization that her secret weapon was missing. She stopped short of mentioning Duke's kiss, however. The experience was still too new, too fresh in her blood to share just yet.

"So Victor turned out to be a cheating scum and a criminal, *and* you lost a video fit for blackmail all in the same day?" Lexi frowned. "Then what's with the dreamy look I'm seeing in your eyes, girlfriend?"

Amanda searched for words, knowing she looked like a fish with her open mouth working soundlessly.

"The cop was a hottie, wasn't he?" Lexi grinned triumphantly, crossing her arms over her angora sweater. "I bet he drooled himself dry if you were wearing some sexy getup for Victor. Did you flash him your garters?"

"Of course not." Amanda sighed, realizing she couldn't hide anything from Lexi. "I wore my coat over my videotape outfit, but I did *not* flash the detective a thing."

"Come on, Amanda. A New York cop doesn't miss a trick. I'll bet he knew exactly what you were wearing underneath that coat and that's why he hit on you."

"He didn't hit on me!"

Lexi leaned forward on the sofa, propping her elbows on her knees. "Please. Every man hits on you until he finds out whose daughter you are." She pointed one dragon-lady nail at Amanda. "But that's what will be great about the cop—no detective worth his badge would shy away from Clyde Matthews's daughter just because of a few mob connections."

"Lex—" Amanda warned.

Lexi, of all people, knew how much her father's friendships with mobsters bothered her. Amanda had vowed to confront her father about it before the busy fashion season got into full swing again in the fall. The thought of a serious talk with her father made her stomach knot as the man had the attention span of a six-year-old and he possessed zero interest in anything that didn't pertain to style or fashion.

"Okay, *rumored* mob connections. This guy could be your ticket to adventure. And he sounds way more fun than stick-in-the-mud Victor ever was."

"Duke doesn't 'sound' like anything, because I haven't told you one thing about him," Amanda hissed before crunching into a gingersnap.

"Ah, but you know my imagination beats the truth of the matter any day." Lexi stole Amanda's other cookie and munched a bite before Amanda's words sank in. "Duke? Did I hear you right that this guy's name is Duke?"

Amanda smiled.

Lexi sighed. "That makes him sound like a German shepherd. Or maybe a prissy English nobleman. I wonder where on earth he got a name like Duke?"

"Trust me, you wouldn't be thinking prissy or canine if you got a look at this guy." Just the thought of Duke Rawlins sent a shiver of anticipation through her. Amanda had never been kissed the way Duke had kissed her. The few sensual encounters she'd had in her life hadn't lit her fire half as much as the simple brush of Duke's mouth on hers.

"So, aren't you a little worried he'll find your video if he's searching Victor's place?" Lexi fed the last crumb of her gingersnap to Muffin, who licked her lips long after she devoured the tiny piece.

A nibble of fear prodded Amanda. "Not really. I mean, I remember feeling it in my pocket when I was seated in the apartment, and then I didn't have it in the cab. So I feel pretty sure I lost it in between the interrogation and the taxi."

Lexi nodded an I-see sort of nod, but she didn't look convinced. Amanda's nibble of fear transformed into an all-out painful bite.

"But if he did happen to find the tape," Lexi continued, "what would he see? I mean, how hot is this secret weapon of yours?"

"It's not so much that the tape is hot. Mortifying is more like it. I'm not exactly a trained exotic dancer." Amanda shivered at the thought of Duke Rawlins seeing her prance around nearly naked, using her limited feminine wiles to entice anyone who happened to view the video. But he *had* said he didn't find anything in the apartment after she left, hadn't he?

"Do tell." Lexi tucked her hair behind an ear and leaned closer. "I'm dying to hear all about your adventures in stripping."

Amanda rolled her eyes. "It was totally hokey. I don't even know if I would have had the nerve to show it to Victor. The tape was more of a Plan B in case the real-life glimpses of lingerie didn't work.''

A wicked grin slid across Lexi's lips. "Did you take it *all* off for the camera?"

Amanda shot her friend a censorious glare and distanced herself from the scandalous conversation by hiding behind her teacup. "I haven't gone *that* far astray. I had no intention of ditching the panties, but I think I did end up exposing a bit more umm... cleavage than I had intended. And I was about as graceful as a preschool ballerina.''

Lexi shook her head, wide-eyed. "I give you credit, Amanda. You're pretty gutsy when it comes to launching your own business or creating knockout clothes. But I never thought you'd really follow through on the striptease plan.''

"Desperate times call for desperate measures.'' Shrugging, Amanda slid more deeply into the leather cushions of the couch, comforted by the soft seat and Lexi's reminder of her recent professional achievements.

Amanda *did* have a lot going for her, even if she'd screwed up today. "Now I'm more desperate than ever since my one and only boyfriend of this decade has been carted off to jail.''

"Except now there's a sexy detective in the picture,'' Lexi reminded her. "Maybe you ought to turn your seductive pursuits to someone on the right side of the law.''

Amanda glowered. "I'm putting my seductive efforts out of commission, thank you very much. I obviously have hideous judgment when it comes to men. I'm not about to go from the frying pan into the fire.''

Lexi might have muttered something to the effect of some people being lucky to find someone to light their fire at all, but Amanda chose to ignore the remark. She would be hard-pressed to remain aloof at her meeting with Duke tomorrow morning, but she was determined to put her attraction to him behind her.

She'd meant it when she told Lexi she couldn't trust her judgment in men. Her track record stunk. Tomorrow, she'd find a way to walk away from Duke Rawlins and his sexy-as-sin blue eyes, no matter how much her hormones protested.

She had every intention of slamming the door on an embarrassing chapter of her life, forgetting that god-awful striptease show ever happened and returning her attention to her designs for the fall line.

And if her existence occasionally seemed a bit sheltered, a little dull? She had the memory of this hideous day to ensure she didn't feel adventurous any time soon.

DUKE ARRIVED AT the precinct late the next morning. He'd spent half the night following a lead on a drug smuggling operation, trailing two suspects through the streets and subway tunnels, only to come up empty-handed. He feared the case was somehow linked to Victor Gallagher's arrest, maybe some cohorts getting antsy now that the cops were cracking down on the Garment District, but he couldn't prove anything. Yet.

The fruitless night only made him more determined than ever to get back to the evidence plucked from Gallagher's apartment. He needed to review everything before Amanda Matthews strolled in with her mile-long legs and her damnably distracting body. The memory of her kiss had kept him awake long after his suspects had fled and he lay in his bed.

He swigged a cup of black coffee from the endless vat of over-brewed station house java. How was it possible that no matter what time he arrived in the morning, the coffee always tasted like liquid soot?

Reaching his desk, he noticed his partner already at his keyboard, a box of tissues at his side. The pink tissues looked at odds with Josh's tough-guy glare and monochromatic dark clothes.

Josh saluted Duke with his mug without looking up.

"You lost the trail last night, man." Josh's hoarse voice made him sound like the Godfather.

The expletive Duke shot back was familiar language around the precinct. "If I'd had your slow butt with me, I never would have been able to tail them for as long as I did. Can I help it they lucked into the A train just before it pulled out of Twenty-third Street?"

"I can hardly expect you to keep up with the Eighth Avenue Express." Josh tore a piece of paper out of the printer and waved it in the air, grinning like a kid holding his first autograph. "But I'll bet you didn't know Gallagher's mother lives in Rockaway. I'm guessing those kids you followed last night are Gallagher recruits, homegrown in his stomping ground. They were probably hightailing it back to Rockaway."

Duke frowned. "Sort of a long shot, huh?"

Josh tugged on his coat and snorted. "I thought your granddaddy taught you to follow your instincts?"

"He also used to say, 'leave no stone unturned,'" Duke quipped.

"The Adage King strikes again." Backing toward the door, Josh pointed to a box on Duke's desk. "I signed out the evidence from Gallagher's apartment for you. Everything's in that box."

Duke flashed him a thumbs-up and headed for the box, his own instincts telling him what to reach for first.

The videotape.

The "Private" label had him curious. Besides, sitting in the media room taking notes would be an easy job while he waited for the caffeine to hit him. He grabbed the video and another cup of the soot elixir, then headed for the viewing room.

He closed the door behind him to shut out the hubbub of the police station. Phones rang off the hook, jailbirds argued with their arresting officers, and panicked citizens reported missing purses, missing bikes and missing people to the desk clerks.

But inside the media room, relative quiet reigned. The room was set up like a small living room complete with two worn couches and a coffee table. Books, maps and other reference materials lined the walls, but the room didn't get used as much since the explosion of the Internet.

Duke sipped his coffee and plugged in the tape. He noted it was already rewound to the beginning. Following his personal standard procedure, he made a quick, high-speed dub of the tape for backup in case the tape got eaten by the media room's equipment. He sank into one of the couches and pulled the coffee table close with the heel of one scuffed loafer. Trading his coffee cup for a yellow legal pad, Duke peered at the screen.

The sight that greeted his eyes assured him he hadn't gotten nearly enough sleep.

A guy had to be dreaming to be seeing socialite Amanda Matthews slithering across the television screen in a black strapless gown with a slit up the side that exposed tantalizing glimpses of skin and....

Was that a garter he'd seen peeking through the slit?

Duke dropped his legal pad and scrambled for the remote. Jabbing the Stop button, Duke transformed the screen from last night's fantasy into static and snow.

This couldn't be happening. The situation mirrored

his dreams too perfectly to be real. Besides, he knew from Amanda's innocent reactions to his kiss yesterday that she was a little on the sheltered side and not exactly well-versed in the art of seduction.

So he was definitely *not* seeing her flashing her pink garters on a videotape he'd found at Victor's home.

Then again, Amanda *had* been the guy's girlfriend.

Duke took a last swig of coffee to steel himself, then pressed the Play button.

Right on cue, Amanda sashayed down a miniature runway with that killer walk of hers, her long legs teasing him via the slit in her gown. He might have written off the footage as a simple video memoir, a glimpse of Amanda getting ready to go out for the evening, if it hadn't been for the tinny music playing in the background. Amanda happened to be strutting her stuff to the beat of "The Stripper," the classic song by Porter or Gershwin or somebody like that.

Heat surged through him. This was no dream. Amanda Matthews began performing a striptease right before his very eyes. This was more than just his lucky day. This coup made his whole damn year.

His mouth went so dry all the coffee in the station wouldn't have been able to cure him.

Sneaking a surreptitious look at the door, Duke jumped off the couch to turn the VCR machine sideways to hide the screen and the revealing evidence from anyone who might venture in the media room. He glared at the window blinds and, wanting to cover all the bases, he pulled them closed. Duke might be stealing an unauthorized glimpse of Amanda, but he'd be damned if he would let anyone else snag a look at this.

For a moment, he considered the ethics of the situation as he settled himself back on the couch. He couldn't deny that watching the Amanda video felt a bit like invading her privacy. But he had obtained the tape as part of his investigation and he needed to know if it contained anything that would incriminate Gallagher.

Maybe if Duke had been a better man, he would have fast-forwarded over Amanda's seductive show. His finger wavered over the Forward button, urging him to do the honorable thing. But just then Amanda turned her back to the camera and reached for the zipper on the back of her gown.

The blood pounded through his veins with an audible swish. The room temperature jumped at least ten degrees. Duke dropped the remote on the coffee table, gladly trading his eligibility for sainthood to watch that zipper slide south.

Inch by tantalizing inch, her skin revealed itself to his avid stare. His eyes tracked her gloved fingers' progress as she slowly tugged the zipper. In his mind's eye, he inserted his hand over hers, his palm against that smooth back. He could practically feel the slide of her satin dress on his knuckles, the warmth of Amanda beneath his fingers. Finally, after he'd held his breath for as long as he possibly could, the expanse of exposed creamy white flesh gave way to the shimmering silk and revealing lace of some hot pink corset kind of thing that sent his jaw to the floor.

Any lethargy he'd felt earlier this morning vanished. Staring at Amanda Matthews made every inch of his body leap to complete, intense alert. Restless tension thrummed through him as she paused her seductive unveiling. The artless way she looked at the camera almost made him think she'd just gotten her zipper stuck. Then out of the blue, her dress gave way beneath her fingers and fell to the runway floor in a pile of rich black satin.

She was beautiful. Not reed thin like some of the fashion-conscious types. No, she had enough curves to make a man want to linger.

He absorbed every inch of Amanda's voluptuous body, from her lace-clad breasts to her gartered thighs, pausing for heart-stopping moments on the places in between.

Her panties complemented the corset, bright pink silk with matching lace. The garters framed the most intriguing portion of those panties, making him wonder what it would be like to touch those bare thighs, to slide his palms over her hips, to smooth his thumbs down the front of her pink silken panties....

The memory of the kiss they'd shared chose that moment to torment him. The knowledge that he'd been kissing this hot-as-a-pistol woman and not just a fashion maven in a conservative trench coat almost proved his undoing. His damn palms were sweaty enough to warrant a swipe across the front of his khakis.

He took deep breaths. He could handle this, couldn't he? After all, he was torturing himself for the sake of police business, right? Yeah, right.

With a superhuman effort, Duke forced himself to note other details about the video besides Amanda Matthews's man-killing sex appeal. First, he noticed the setting—a loft with big windows and hardwood floors. Against his will, his eye strayed back to Amanda's legs, the sheer pink stockings niggling at his brain and distracting him at the same time. He closed his eyes and opened them again, trying valiantly to see around her gorgeous self.

The only thing relevant that came to mind was that the video's unfamiliar surroundings meant it hadn't been filmed at Victor's place.

Yet Victor had seen it.

The knowledge that the tape had been made for another man and not for him served as a mental cold shower and gave Duke a tiny measure of control back.

Amanda would no doubt be horrified to know Duke had ever seen her "Private" video. Not that her comfort was uppermost in his mind. No matter how horrified she might be, Duke would give her the tape back. Although he'd have to bend procedural rules to deliver the video to her, there wasn't a chance in hell he would bring the tape back to the evidence room and risk someone else seeing Amanda at her mouth-watering best.

He would give this tantalizing morsel back to Amanda right after he watched the rest. He needed to make sure there was nothing incriminating in it before he broke—er, bended—police regulation.

Duke shifted in his seat, willing away his body's alert state. This was a hell of a position to be in during working hours. He tried not to think about Amanda's seductive little shimmy as she clicked her way back up the runway and tossed her gloves in either direction.

He had to smile that Amanda wore gloves and an evening gown for a striptease. She was a throwback to a pinup girl with her teasing strut and her decadent clothes. All she needed was a bubble machine to complete the image. She lacked the in-your-face sexuality of the women in today's strip joints, but to his way of thinking, she was ten times as tempting.

As if to challenge the truth of his thoughts, Amanda slowly began to unlace the ties of the lingerie. She wound one cord around her finger until the string went taut, and then pulled.

Perhaps she had misjudged how much pressure the flimsy garment had been under, because the moment the restraining knot slipped free, the ribbons slithered all the way out of position and sent her lingerie sliding downward.

Duke forgot all pretense of noting anything else but Amanda. His eyes sought a glimpse of her breasts as diligently as a teenager searching for nipples in a bra commercial. And this time, his keen eyes locked on just what he sought.

An unimpeded view of one rounded, lush breast, naked and seemingly…aroused.

A lesser man might have pressed the Pause button.

Duke would have if he hadn't heard an ominous pair of high heels clicking down the long hall toward the media room through the closed door.

Damn.

Duke leaped off the couch, remembering his eleven o'clock appointment with the stripteasing star of the "Private" videotape.

He bolted over to the VCR and hit Eject but not before he had a chance to see one final glimpse of a half-naked Amanda Matthews before she strutted away from the camera. The blush flamed on her cheeks, her arms folded carefully over her breasts and impossibly high-heeled Barbie doll shoes hugged her feet.

Barbie doll shoes?

Duke had tied those same insubstantial pink heels to her feet with his own hands yesterday.

How in the hell could he get himself under control to question Amanda when he had just guessed exactly what Miss High Society had been wearing under her conservative trench coat yesterday morning?

Absolutely nothing.

5

AMANDA STRODE DOWN a long corridor of Duke's police station wearing the fourth dress she'd tried on that morning. It had been too warm out for the full body armor she'd probably need to rein in her reaction to him, so she'd settled for a conservative pink sheathe dress and the extra layer of her trench coat.

The din of the station house clamored around her, punctuated by ringing phones, raised voices and raucous byplay among the policemen and women. She might have located Duke sooner if it hadn't been for the dozen officers who interrupted her progress to make sure she knew where she was going. By the time a grizzled desk sergeant offered to escort her to Duke himself, Amanda had the impression the tenth precinct didn't receive many noncriminal visitors.

They certainly were a courteous lot.

She nodded at whatever the smiling sergeant was saying, too nervous about her upcoming meeting to pay attention to the man's monologue about the police station.

What would Duke want to ask her about? She hoped he wouldn't continue questioning her charac- ter. It had been humiliating enough to learn her boyfriend was a criminal without some too-brash detective asking her if she did drugs. What must he think of her?

Of course, Duke Rawlins wouldn't have kissed her yesterday if he'd believed her to be some sort of delinquent, right?

She gulped back her apprehension and steeled herself as her escort rapped on a closed door and then opened it partway.

She heard the man call into the room. "Rawlins, I've got a young lady out here looking for you." The sergeant nodded and then turned to Amanda. "He's in here. Nice to meet you, Ms. Matthews."

Amanda reciprocated the compliment, wishing she could be questioned by a nice, neutral third party like the sergeant instead of a flashy detective who seemed oblivious to the concept of personal boundaries. Still, she nodded her thanks and stepped inside the room.

Her first thought was that they were all alone—something she definitely hadn't counted on. Her second thought centered on her interrogator and the fact that he looked at her with predatory, knowing eyes. Amanda shivered, distracting herself by peering around the room.

A dated sofa set dominated the small space. A coffee table lurked in the middle covered with newspapers and a blank legal pad. Shelves full of reference materials ringed the walls except for the wall that contained a window. Duke stood at the window now, opening the blinds to flood the room with late morning sun.

The light helped alleviate the sense of intimacy, but it also seemed to heighten her awareness and sharpen her perception of Duke now that she could see him clearly.

He wore a gray T-shirt with a blue and silver star emblazoned across his chest. A logo loomed underneath the image and the design seemed to be a team shirt of some sort, but Amanda couldn't help but note the recurring theme in his wardrobe.

No matter what Lexi said, however, the man did *not* render her starry-eyed. A little hot under the merry widow, maybe, but not starry-eyed.

Oh God. Did she really just think that?

"Good morning." Duke greeted her in a husky voice that made her wonder what it would be like to hear those words across a pillow instead of across a shabby interrogation room.

"Hi." Amanda forced herself to meet his gaze, no matter how much it scorched right through her. She would answer his questions and then she would bolt. She'd had enough adventure yesterday to last her for at least a few years. She didn't need the star-spangled hotshot to lead her further astray. When she wasn't busy dating criminals or making illicit home videos, she had a fledgling business to run, after all.

"Can I take your coat?"

His question seemed innocuous enough, but that sexy rasp in his voice unnerved her.

"No, thanks." The temperature had already soared in the room, but Amanda opted to keep her coat for security's sake. Once she started shedding clothes around this man, there was no telling when she might stop.

As if sensing her thoughts, Duke's gaze tripped down her body, her simple crepe dress with its ankle-grazing hem revealed by her open coat. Amanda fidgeted under his scrutiny.

"Have a seat," he offered, moving around the furniture to gesture toward the couch. He shuffled a stack of things on the coffee table, his legal pad and maybe a book underneath it, then shoved aside the TV/VCR cart someone had pulled right up to the seating area.

They both took a seat then and stared at each other for one awkward moment. Amanda had promised herself she would not think about that kiss while in his presence, but in that heated exchange of glances she found her gaze darting toward his lips. His mouth had been a sensual discovery for her, nothing like what she'd ever experienced before.

Duke cleared his throat and drummed his fingers on the legal pad. "I only have a couple of questions for you, Amanda, so I'll try to make this quick."

Giving herself a mental shake, Amanda sat up straighter, needing to get this final encounter out of the way. She had a safe life to return to, after all. "I'm ready."

His blue eyes locked on hers. "Did you have an intimate relationship with Gallagher?"

She flew off the couch, utterly unsettled, and maybe even outraged. "What kind of question is that?"

He remained in his seat. "A professional one, Amanda. I have a reason for asking, which I'll get around to in a minute. For now, could you please answer the question?" His voice remained cool and aloof, lending credence to his words. "And it's important you be honest with me on this."

The last comment nettled. He questioned her integrity?

"No, I was not intimate with Victor." Her cheeks burned at the admission. Not that she was necessarily embarrassed for Duke to learn as much, but just that they would be discussing such a thing at all. As an afterthought, she added, "But I was working on it."

Duke's mouth seemed to fall open of its own accord, but it took him a moment to find a response. "You were working on it?"

She'd be damned if she would explain any more than that, so she offered him a curt nod.

He shook his head, his eyes skimming every inch of her. "I wouldn't think a woman like you would have to work at it too hard, Amanda."

His veiled compliment ignited a surge of feminine pride. Why did this presumptuous badge-wielding renegade have the power to make her feel outrageously sexy with just one comment? She'd pranced around a runway in little more than her garters yesterday before she went over to Victor's and the experience hadn't been nearly as titillating as Duke's lone observation.

While Amanda struggled to find a graceful way to move the conversation forward, Duke pulled something out from under his legal pad and passed it across the coffee table to her. "Tell me, Amanda, did you use this to convince him to cross the line?"

Still reeling from a heady dose of sexual attraction, Amanda's eyes fluttered over the object in his hand for a moment before realizing what he was trying to hand her.

One videotape labeled "Private."

Amanda might have been embarrassed if she hadn't been so consumed by righteous indignation. The blue-eyed traitor had her secret weapon all along.

"How dare you!" Amanda snatched the world's lone recording of her amateurish attempt at a striptease out of Duke's hand. "I thought you said you didn't find anything of mine in Victor's apartment?" She allowed her words to convey all the betrayal she felt.

"Did I say that?" He squinted his eyes as if genuinely attempting to recall his words. "Well I sure as hell didn't suspect this was yours since you told me you lost a date book and not a videotape."

Her lie chastened her somewhat, because she truly *hadn't* wanted to lie to a police detective, but this was still his fault. "I could hardly tell you the truth."

"I don't care for being lied to, Amanda," his gaze was stark and serious for all of a millisecond before his blue eyes scorched her with their heat. "But I can't exactly say I was disappointed with what I discovered because you lied."

Her heart started a slow thump of dread, realizing he had probably watched her shameless show. Winging a quick prayer her secret hadn't been fully revealed, Amanda lifted the video to study the length of tape on each reel. Three quarters of the tape rested in the right-hand widow of the cassette, indicating the viewer had indeed watched the whole thing.

Including the accidental peep show at the end.

Amanda felt the steam build between her ears, but she couldn't deny the curious heat pricking along the rest of her, too. Duke Rawlins had seen her practically naked.

She blinked quickly, willing away images of Duke watching her on-screen. She didn't want to know what he thought of her show. Did she? Then why did the thought of him seeing her in the buff make her blood simmer in her veins?

This was not good.

Squelching all thoughts of arousal she jammed the tape in her trench coat pocket, back where it belonged. "You only had to look at five seconds worth of footage on this tape to figure out it belonged to me."

Duke flashed her an unrepentant grin. "Honey, it only took five seconds worth of footage to glue me to my chair."

Amanda's pulse jumped into overdrive. She'd tried

to brainwash herself on the cab ride to the station this morning with the ''I'm not going to get too close to Duke Rawlins'' mantra. But here she was, getting sucked in by that blue-eyed charm and those delicious pecs all over again.

She fought off his seductive pull by arguing with him. ''You didn't need to move, all you needed to do was click the remote. And don't even tell me you didn't have it available, because from what I can gather, men aren't capable of watching television without the remote control in hand.''

He leaned across the table and lowered his voice to a sexy whisper. ''Once I got turned on, I couldn't turn it off.''

Amanda had to sit on her hands to keep from fanning herself. The man was too much, too hot, too soon. Too bad she found herself wrapped up in that throaty whisper, ready to hear more about his reaction to her tape.

If he wanted to flirt with her, who was she to refuse? Maybe it was time she hauled out the real Amanda.

Duke watched a confusing array of emotion pass through Amanda's eyes and tried to calculate her response. He wasn't sure how far he could push her, and he didn't want her to bolt.

But how could he resist flirting with her just a little? Her striptease still scorched through his memory, superimposing itself across the present to tease and tempt him. Images of her creamy thighs sheathed in sheer pink stockings threatened to obliterate his awareness of the police station and the damn questioning.

The questioning.

Duke sat up straighter, needing to put this meeting behind him. Or at least get his questions answered so he could move on to exploring other, more interesting terrain with Ms. Matthews.

The only thing he really cared about investigating right now was what Amanda might be wearing beneath her clothes today. But Duke Rawlins prided himself on his ability not to get distracted on the job.

Yeah, right.

He cleared his throat and scrambled for a stabilizing breath of air. "So you never answered my question."

Amanda reached her hand underneath her long hair and tossed it over one shoulder. "There was a question in there? I thought you were trying to torment me with reminders that you've watched my...show."

Torment was definitely not on his list of things to do with this woman if he ever got the chance. But if he didn't get this questioning back on semiprofessional footing, he'd be in trouble. "I meant my earlier question. Did you bring this tape to Gallagher's hoping to—" He searched for a way to frame the question. "—foster an intimate relationship?"

She sat up straighter. Her eyes narrowed. "Does this question have anything to do with police business?"

"If you didn't have an intimate relationship with Gallagher, it makes me less inclined to think you were associated with his crimes." He wouldn't have revealed as much if he wasn't pretty damn sure his instincts were correct. But once he'd recalled discovering the video in her chair, it only made sense that she'd just brought it over that day. Especially in light of the intriguing outfit he was positive she'd been wearing under her trench coat.

Amanda frowned. "I made the video yesterday morning and brought it to his house hoping to incite—"

She paused so long, Duke couldn't restrain himself. "Lust?" he prompted.

She cast him a reproving glare. "Male interest. But I obviously needn't have bothered as Victor was spending all his male interest elsewhere."

Satisfaction rolled over Duke like a sunny day. By opting to arrest Vic yesterday, he'd not only put away a criminal, he'd saved Amanda the indignation of wasting her considerable charms on an unworthy man. He mentally chalked up two stars for that particular good deed.

"Amanda, I have no doubt Gallagher would have been very 'male interested' in your video, but between you and me, I'm glad he never got to see it." Maybe it wasn't exactly a professional comment. But this wasn't exactly a *formal* questioning anyway.

He was gratified to see a little of the starch fade from her spine.

She flashed him a conspiratorial smile that made him feel like a damn hero. "Me, too. I'm definitely glad Mr. Cheating Silk Suit never got so much as a glimpse of me." In a familiar gesture, she tugged her coat a bit closer. "Are we done talking about him?"

Duke didn't really want to talk about her ex-boyfriend or the investigation, either. Especially given that Amanda could still be a part of a bigger crime picture. She seemed less guilty now that he'd realized she wasn't as close to Gallagher as he'd originally thought. Then again, she had proven she wasn't afraid to lie to a cop to save her own skin.

He nodded. "I am hoping you'll testify for me if I need you to, however."

"I don't know anything about him smuggling drugs," she protested.

"No, but you can tell a judge all about how he tried to get a jump on knowing what fabrics to send to your father. He shipped the drugs in with the bolts of material, you know." Would she try to extract herself from acting as a witness? Maybe her father wouldn't like her ratting out one of his cohorts.

Amanda nodded. "I'd be happy to testify."

Duke's respect for her jumped another notch, but now that they'd sewn up business details, he had to admit he mourned the loss of the innuendo-laden conversation they had indulged in earlier.

He didn't want to get involved with another woman who ran in high-society circles, but memories of Amanda's deliciously amateur striptease still teased him. He'd never forget the slow seduction of her zipper sliding downward, the moment the black satin pooled at her feet.

Maybe that's why words started falling off his tongue before he could halt them. "Then I guess we're all set here. Can I walk you out?"

Rising from the shabby media-room couch, Amanda looked wary, but she nodded. "Okay."

Duke guided her out of the building, ignoring the blatant attempts of his co-workers angling for an introduction. He wasn't about to share his last few minutes with Amanda.

He held the front door for her, stepping out into the warm spring sunlight. Squad cars lined up out front, ready to leave at a moment's notice. For now, the street was quiet, however, and Duke found himself steering her toward one of the parked cars.

For reasons he couldn't quite comprehend, he wasn't ready to say goodbye to Amanda yet. The permanent replay of her video in his mind definitely didn't help. He would *not* stoop so low as to undress her with his eyes, but could he help it if he had a full-color image of her gartered thighs and bare breasts tattooed on the back of his eyelids?

As if reading his mind, Amanda patted the steamy video in her pocket. "Thanks for returning this to me."

He'd have to come up with a whopper of an excuse for the missing evidence, but it would be worth the smile on her face. The need to kiss her again, to taste the lips that could make him forget his own name, overwhelmed him. "No problem. I really did need to watch it in case it contained other evidence."

The wind lifted a strand of her hair to wave like a flag across her cheek. Amanda absently tucked it behind her ear. "It's okay. I would have honestly been more upset if you hadn't found this at Victor's and he'd discovered it himself. I would be mortified to have him see how close I'd come to—you know—with him." She twisted and twirled the belt that dangled from her coat.

Warmth unfurled in Duke's chest along with a surge of protectiveness. "Does that mean I'm forgiven for indulging in your show?"

The bright sunlight showed a delicate pink blush on Amanda's cheeks. Her brown eyes glinted with mischief as she whipped her coat's belt in a little circle like a Ferris wheel at her waist. "Do you promise not to tell?"

Duke felt like a sucker fish with his mouth wide open and waiting for the hook. No matter how much he spouted about keeping away from the wayward society women, this particular female had the power to reel him in for as long as she wanted. "Honey, I'm happy to keep as many secrets as you care to reveal."

He couldn't help it that his gaze wandered over her body. Had he really said he would never undress her with his eyes?

She laughed and idly whipped his arm with the

cloth belt of her coat. "You are a scandal waiting to happen, Detective Rawlins."

He wanted to still her nervous hands and shifting feet with a kiss that would render her senseless. He settled for flirting with her instead, wondering what had gotten into him that he was pursuing a woman who would be exactly all wrong for him.

"You should talk, Ms. Matthews." He took a step closer, observing the way she backed into the door of a parked squad car. "I'd say you were the scandal waiting to happen if I'm right about what you were wearing beneath that coat yesterday."

Her hands freed the belt she'd been holding and fluttered idly in front of his chest. She shot him a none-too-innocent glance. "I'm not sure I know what you mean."

"I thought maybe it was just wishful thinking when I caught a glimpse of stocking up around your thigh." He didn't dare step any closer, but he trailed his finger across her thigh in just the right spot, telling himself maybe she needed a visual to refresh her memory. "But then when I watched the video I realized exactly what you were hiding from me."

Amanda's flesh tingled, trembled and tightened where Duke had touched her through her thin crepe skirt. Heat pulsed through her legs, compromising her ability to stand without wavering.

She leaned more heavily against the police car, considering the wisdom of baiting the man but powerless to stop herself. "What do you think I was hiding?"

His big shoulders angled over hers, drawing his chest into agonizingly touchable range. She remembered how it felt to be crushed up against his solid, unforgiving body. She wanted nothing so much as to put herself there again.

But he didn't touch her. He merely breathed his response into her ear. "I think you were hiding the real you."

Her heart hammered in her chest as if clamoring to be heard. She'd expected him to take their flirtation to the next level, to use her provocation as an excuse to kiss her. She definitely didn't expect to be unveiled at a deeper level.

"I—" She faltered, thinking the time had come to cut and run. Much as she would have liked a few more thought-stealing kisses, she was beginning to feel very out of her league with this man.

"Go out with me, Amanda." He barred her retreat with his big body and his direct approach.

She shook her head automatically, more equipped to take on his brute strength than his brash invitation.

"Why not?" He tipped her chin so she couldn't avoid looking at him. "I happen to know your Saturdays are now free. Spend tomorrow with me."

Amanda scrolled through a mental list of excuses. But mostly, she was afraid theirs was the kind of attraction that could flame out of control with little more than a few kisses.

"I need to attend a dinner tomorrow night," she finally managed.

Unfazed, Duke smiled. "Great. That means you have the afternoon to spend with me. I'll bet an uptown girl like you hardly ever has the pleasure of venturing downtown on a Saturday."

A daytime date? Amanda didn't think that would really help take the focus off sex at all. It was broad daylight now, with yellow cabs racing past and pedestrians crowding the sidewalk, and she couldn't seem to think about anything else. "I don't know—"

"I bet a woman with your eye for design would love a day on Canal Street. We'll hit all the cool vendors and then I'll buy you an ice cream to atone for watching the video. You'll be home in plenty of time for your dinner."

She had to admit it sounded like fun. Still, Amanda wouldn't make the mistake of underestimating Duke. No matter how many ice-cream cones you stuffed in the man's hand, he still generated enough heat to put Amanda in meltdown mode. "Thanks, but I don't think it's a good idea for us to see each other again."

He leaned close to her again, curse his eyes, and shook her determination to smithereens. "The woman I saw in your video wasn't afraid to take chances."

His blue gaze told her he'd studied her every move on that tape, had read into everything she'd wanted to convey about herself, and maybe a little she hadn't meant to.

Amanda folded her arms across her chest in a belated attempt to insert some space between them. "That woman made a big mistake."

"That woman wasn't scared to go after what she wanted," he corrected.

"No offense, Duke, but I don't know that I want you."

His knowing grin told her his years on the force had probably turned him into a walking lie detector. "What about that kiss yesterday? I'm thinking you told me something else while we were kissing each other like there was no tomorrow."

He had a point there.

"Well—"

"Why don't we meet in Battery Park at noon? We'll do the whole thing on neutral territory and you leave when you want to."

Truth be told, she didn't have a dinner appointment tomorrow. She had nothing to do tomorrow, except maybe obsess about the next showing of her new collection. Duke Rawlins's offer sounded like more fun than stalking around her loft getting an ulcer while she worried.

Besides, hadn't she wanted a little adventure in her life?

"Okay."

She hadn't been prepared for him to grab the loose ties of her coat and pull her forward, but that's exactly what he did.

He kissed her once with a slow but assertive sweep of his tongue then set her aside. "Excellent."

She couldn't tell if that was approval for the kiss or for agreeing to the date, but she felt a smile tug at her mouth either way.

Amanda stepped away from the police car and backed down the street. "So noon tomorrow?"

He nodded. "And Amanda?"

She paused.

"Don't forget to bring the real you."

DUKE ENJOYED WATCHING her walk away.

No matter that she'd glowered at him. She'd agreed to see him again.

He retreated into the police station once she was out of sight, carefully squelching the urge to whistle. He wanted to shout his victory from the rooftops but he wouldn't do it for the viewing pleasure of the tenth precinct.

Successfully dodging the idly curious cops who'd watched him walk out with Amanda, Duke navigated his way back to the media room to snag his extra copy of Amanda's sexy tape. Soon he would destroy it. But he would lock it in his desk until after Gallagher's sentencing came down. As much as Duke fancied himself an honorable guy for giving Amanda her original tape back, professional instincts told him to keep the backup copy just in case it contained some clue he wasn't yet aware of.

He slapped the tape against his thigh in a double-time rhythm as he strode back down the hallway to his desk. Prepared to delve into the remaining evidence in the Gallagher case, he halted when he saw Josh sprawled in his office chair, his boots looking quite at home on Duke's desk.

Duke nudged his partner's feet off his Mets' desk calendar while he locked Amanda's tape into his top drawer with the other hand. "Don't tell me you've been to Queens and are back already."

"How many hours did you think it would take?" Josh didn't look up, but continued leafing through a sheaf of computer printouts. "Maybe you just lost track of the time while you were charming your way into bed with the mafia princess."

Duke's good mood slipped a few rungs. "You got a bone to pick, Winger?"

Josh shuffled his papers into a pile and stood. "No. Just surprised to see you hovering around Gallagher's girlfriend out front. You sure you know what you're getting into, Rawlins?"

Of course he didn't know what he was getting into. He'd asked Amanda out based on gut instincts instead of logic. "Maybe not. But I'm going to have a fine time finding out."

Josh shook his head. "Your granddaddy ever tell you the one about 'look before you leap'?"

Only every other day. But he wasn't owning up to that one. "Granddaddy was more of a 'don't let the grass grow under your feet' kind of guy." Agitated, Duke plucked up a blue stress management ball someone had given him as a gag gift and tossed it from hand to hand.

Josh clapped him on the shoulder and stalked toward his own desk. Over his shoulder he called, "Maybe you should worry more about the grass that'll be growing over your head when you're six feet under, buddy. I hear those mob bosses don't take kindly to cops who make moves on their daughters."

"There's a cheery thought. Thanks, Winger." Duke tossed his stress management ball at Josh's retreating shoulder.

It bounced off his oversize partner and fell to the floor.

Damn it all, Duke didn't feel so much like whistling now.

6

AMANDA GRIPPED THE rail of the barricade standing between her and the New York Harbor. Wind blew in off the water, tossing her hair about her shoulders and wreaking havoc with her long cotton skirt.

The Staten Island Ferry sat at one end of Battery Park, the Ellis Island Ferry at the other. Amanda had arrived early to meet Duke and had already scoped out the terrain.

He'd been correct in his assumption that she didn't venture downtown too often. Her world had grown insular in these last few years with her relentless pursuit of her career.

But she needed to get out more. The half hour she'd spent people watching and strolling around on her own had inspired design ideas to keep her busy for the next month.

She stuffed some change in one of the stationary binoculars and looked out over the harbor, thinking she at least owed Duke a thank-you for coercing her into an outing. She could indulge in a small escapade today and be home before dinner. What would it hurt?

Ducking her head to line up her eyes with the viewing windows, Amanda assured herself she could walk away from Duke today. She'd been craving adventure, but to see Duke on a regular basis would be more adventure than she could handle.

She squinted to see a view of the harbor but the only thing she could glimpse through the eyepiece was a bright blue star.

A sexy baritone drifted on the breeze. "Hey, gorgeous. See anything you like in there?"

Amanda couldn't help but smile. She peered over the binocular stand to see Duke Rawlins, his spiky hair headed in various directions, his blue T-shirt blank except for five stars in a horizontal line across it. "How could I not like a man with a five-star rating?"

"You're a woman with discriminating taste." Duke tucked a stray strand of her windblown hair behind her ear and eyed her warily. "Are you sure you're ready to hit Canal Street with me and let me junk up that tasteful sophistication of yours?"

"You're not going to send me home in a tourist T-shirt or anything, are you?"

He tugged her hand to pull her forward through the park. "Only if it's mine."

Amanda rather enjoyed the warmth of that strong hand around hers. Duke had a way of imparting a sense of adventure, a feeling that something fun was right around the corner.

"You make some pretty bold statements, Detective," she chided him, unable to dismiss thoughts of herself wrapped in Duke's clothes.

He drew her toward the street and hailed a cab with one wave of his long arm. "My granddaddy used to say 'virtue is bold and goodness never fearful.'"

She slid into the taxicab as he held the door open for her. "Your grandfather liked Shakespeare?"

Duke frowned as he slid in beside her. "Is that Shakespeare?" He directed the cabdriver and then settled back against the seat for the ride. "Guess Granddad was more uptown than I gave him credit for. He mostly absorbed pithy sayings to bombard me with so maybe I'd remember a little of his wisdom when he wasn't around."

Duke's words resounded in his head, sinking into his skull for a change. It amazed him how the older he got, the smarter his crafty grandsire became. Damn it, all these years after the old man's death, he still remembered the wisdom.

"Are you close to your family?" Amanda asked, plucking at the airy cotton skirt she wore.

As usual, she looked great in a unique way, her full, creamy-colored skirt the kind of thing girls in Elvis movies wore with saddle shoes. The yellow silk tank she wore was simple and uncomplicated however, along with the strappy yellow sandals on her feet. Pink painted toenails peeked out of her shoes, as perfect as every other inch of her.

"I've got a couple of brothers I don't see too often, but we were pretty close growing up." The silence seemed more pronounced in light of the street cacophony all around them. The rumble of other cars' engines filtered through the cab's partially open windows, along with the honking that seemed to accompany every other traffic light. "My mom and dad died in a carjacking in Mexico a few weeks after I was born."

Amanda murmured the right sympathetic stuff that Duke never paid attention to. Sure he hated what had happened to his parents, but he'd still had a great home life—light-years better than the homes of the kids he arrested on a regular basis.

Duke had been lucky enough to have his grandfather to keep him on the straight and narrow. Too many kids these days didn't have anyone.

"My mom died when I was five, but at least I had my dad. He's always been busy with his business, but he found ways to make sure I knew he was thinking of me." She winked at Duke across the bench seat. "I was the only girl at boarding school with my own sewing kit, a toy cappuccino maker and a beret. My father said those things would carry me through any crisis."

"Did they?" He couldn't imagine that being shipped off to boarding school would make a little girl who'd lost her mother feel all that loved, but what did he know?

She laughed. "You'd be amazed at how popular you can be at an all-girls school if you know how to make doll clothes. I was a definite hit."

They pulled up to Canal Street and Duke started to hand the cabdriver the fare when Amanda elbowed her way next to him with money in hand. "Here you go."

Duke folded her fingers over her money and edged away the offering. "Subway rides are on you. I'm getting this one."

"I'll get the next cab," Amanda corrected him. "No subways for me on the weekend. I take the trains all week so I can afford to treat myself on the weekend."

"Fair enough." He jumped out of the taxi and held the door for her. He might not come from her swanky side of town, but he considered himself a gentleman, after all.

"Wow." Amanda halted when she got to the street and noticed the long rows of vendors outside the storefronts.

Did it look like one big junk shop to her eyes? She probably shopped Fifth Avenue and Rodeo Drive. Then again, maybe these fashion types didn't shop at all. For all Duke knew, maybe they just dressed themselves in the clothes they designed.

He didn't know what had possessed him to bring her here. Could be some inner demon had wanted him to show her in no uncertain terms that he was a downtown type of guy. His Saturdays were about listening to some good street musicians and walking around Central Park, not sipping champagne in the penthouse suite.

"What do you think?" he finally prompted, wondering if those strappy yellow sandals were going to sprint after the departing taxicab any moment.

Her shoes started clicking, but not in the direction he'd feared. She made a beeline for a vending stand dripping with tacky costume jewelry.

"You have gorgeous merchandise," she gushed to the person behind the counter, an older woman with half glasses perched on her nose who looked like she knew how to spot a sucker at twenty paces.

Duke should have warned her the best bargains went to the best hagglers, but maybe Amanda Matthews didn't ever worry about her bank account.

Then again, she *did* take the subway all week. Maybe she wasn't living off her father's dirty money.

He tugged her aside with an apologetic smile to the eager vendor. "Amanda, can we have a word?"

Begrudgingly, she relinquished a serpent pin covered in green stones and followed him a few steps away. "What?"

He laid his arm over her shoulder, partially to enhance the privacy of their conversation, but mostly because he wanted to touch her. "You know you have to haggle with these people to get a fair price?"

The yellow silk of her blouse fluttered against his skin, teasing his senses and urging him to linger.

The shrewd glint in her narrowed gaze wasn't half as inviting, however. "I've haggled for my father's fabric in more countries than I can count. Trust me, I know what I'm doing."

Duke considered her words, suspecting she was

still a rookie. She'd probably only been able to use her skills at sophisticated foreign trade shows where exorbitant markups might allow for a little genteel dickering. "You've got a highly unorthodox method, you know," he remarked, not wanting to offend her, but not wanting her to get taken for a mint, either.

"You mean my raving about the merchandise?" Amanda whispered, sneaking a longing look at the jewelry over her shoulder.

At least she understood where she was going wrong. Maybe there was still hope for her. "Exactly. You'll never get them to budge on the price if they think you really want something."

She wriggled out from under his arm to stand toe-to-toe with him. Gently, she poked him in the chest with one lacquered pink fingernail. "Watch and learn, Duke. I'll put on a much better show for you today than anything you ever saw on that sordid video-tape."

His eyes dipped to her legs of their own volition. Her teasing words affected him more than a silken stroke to an erogenous zone.

Duke tugged her closer before she could sashay away, unwilling to let her remark pass without a suit-able payback. "Honey, there's nothing I'd like more, but do you think that's such a good idea?" He lowered his head to speak into her ear. The soft length of her hair brushed his cheek. "I'd rather be your only audience."

Perhaps her mental picture of that scenario was as

enticing as his, because she swayed on her feet for one heated moment. Then she backed away, shaking her head and an accusing finger at him.

"That was a mistake, remember? I might have had faulty judgment on the video debacle, but I'm in my element now. How about I meet you down by the pretzel stand after I get warmed up here?"

Duke nodded, very much in favor of seeing Amanda in warmed-up mode. He bought an iced espresso and hung out near a guitar player on the street corner, soaking in the music and sunshine while he watched Amanda move from table to table. Duke smiled to see her in action.

Within twenty minutes she had vendors practically begging her to buy something. Her method was unique but very effective—she knew the power of walking away. He, too, mourned the sight of Amanda walking away, even though the view from behind her was spectacular.

She hadn't been kidding, she was no novice to this game. But he'd be willing to bet she'd never bartered for items quite like Canal Street offered. She moved in circles of the fashion elite and he doubted she bought knockoff sunglasses and rhinestone toe rings when she conducted her father's fabric buying sprees.

He tossed a couple of dollars in the guitar player's hat and moved farther down the street, making sure Amanda didn't get too far away from him. Her latest coup seemed to be a pile of frothy-looking scarves in enough colors to rival a crayon box. He watched her smile and thank the young man who'd sold them to her for a song. The poor sap behind the counter looked as smitten as Duke felt.

Damn.

He chugged the rest of the espresso and wondered why it seemed so right in his gut to be with Amanda, yet so wrong to his head. Even Josh thought he was making a colossal mistake—the same one he'd made before when he got involved with a socialite looking for adventure—yet he stood here with his eyes glued to Amanda Matthews, hungry for an excuse to touch her again, desperate to betray his own ethics and sneak a peek at the video striptease calling to him from his desk drawer at the precinct.

He didn't know how this day would end, but one thing was clear to him as Amanda's laughter floated to him on the warm breeze.

He couldn't let her walk away just yet.

AMANDA SENSED DUKE'S presence behind her long before he touched her. She could tell by the way the woman at the vintage clothing counter fluffed her hair, by the way the air took on a heated quality, the way a ghost of anticipation drifted over Amanda's skin.

Her desire for Duke confused her. She knew better than to get caught up in a relationship that couldn't lead anywhere. The complications of her father's lifestyle, his rumored connections to the mob, would make a relationship with a New York police detective very awkward. She knew her father didn't participate in anything illegal, but he'd cast a pall over their whole family name with his public fraternizing with crime figures.

She needed to tackle that situation before the fall fashion shows started. But not quite yet, not when their talk would inevitably lead to her quitting the window designing work all together. Her father had recently broken up with a long-term girlfriend and his business had been losing money lately. What if her dad perceived Amanda's perspective as hostile, somehow? She couldn't bear a rift with her only living relative.

It was much more pleasant to think about Duke Rawlins's proximity behind her. From the gooseflesh that broke out over her skin at his mere presence, Amanda knew they were already treading on dangerous water.

Today, she didn't care.

His hands settled over the bared part of her shoulders, his thumbs slipping beneath the fabric of her silk tank top. The gesture felt incredibly intimate, the gentle scrape of Duke's hands kneading her sunwarmed skin, but the woman behind the counter merely smiled at them as if nothing were amiss.

Amanda thought about stepping back a few more inches and what it would feel like to be folded against Duke's chest. She had no doubt those five stars on his T-shirt were accurate. From the kiss they'd already shared, Amanda knew sex with Duke would be off the charts.

He brushed his fingers idly over her upper arms. "You were right."

She found it difficult to concentrate on whether she wanted the antique beaded purse or the studded pink evening gloves. "I was?"

"You did put on quite a show today, even without," he leaned fractionally closer and whispered, "getting naked."

Oh my, the man was too much. Too bold. Too brash. Too sexy for her own good.

Amanda forgot all about haggling. The wheeling and dealing game she normally enjoyed paled in comparison to the thrill Duke Rawlins could give her with one seductive whisper.

She handed over a few bills to the woman behind the counter for the purse and the evening gloves.

Duke plucked up one pink glove. "This has burlesque written all over it. I hope you got them with me in mind."

Amanda took it away from him, stuffing it in a sack along with her other purchases. "I got them to show on the runway with next spring's collection. I have a few pieces in mind that are vaguely retro and I think these will help capitalize on the look."

Automatically, Duke took her shopping bag from her. Amanda smiled at his manners, so different from her father's or even Victor's. They could probably order wine in a dozen languages and know how to get a table at any restaurant in New York, but they didn't take care of details like lugging her bags around for her. At best, Victor might have snapped his fingers at his driver to come take her purchases from her.

Obviously, Duke's granddad knew how to raise a gentleman.

He steered her down the street now, where they passed a mime and a juggler. The spring weather seemed to have called out every form of street performer and shopper in the city and Canal Street swelled to overflowing with the growing crush.

"Have you shopped enough yet?" Duke asked, pausing by a stand full of neckties before urging her forward again.

Amanda nodded even though she hated the thought of ending the day. She'd had a great time, but she hadn't really seen much of Duke. Maybe somewhere in her fantasies she'd nursed a hope this day would at least provide her with a few more steal-your-breath kisses for her memory bank. "I guess I'd better get going."

"And miss the zoo?" Duke looked appalled.

"What zoo?" Amanda definitely didn't remember any trips to the zoo in their plans.

Duke guided her toward the street and flagged a taxi. The cab screeched to a halt beside them.

"The Central Park Zoo." He held the door for her and waved her into the waiting car. "I promised you an ice-cream cone, remember? Didn't I mention we were going to eat it at the zoo?''

Relieved she didn't have to leave just yet, and impressed he hadn't pressed for an invitation to her loft, Amanda slid across the black vinyl seat.

''You definitely didn't mention a zoo, but never let it be said I don't have a sense of adventure.''

SEATED ON A bench by the lion exhibit, Duke deeply regretted his sense of adventure as he watched Amanda's tongue navigate the top of her Death by Chocolate ice-cream cone.

How would he ever survive all three scoops?

He struggled to come up with a new conversation starter. When Amanda released a supremely contented sigh over her ice cream, Duke launched into the first thing that came to his mind. ''So have you lived in the loft over your father's showroom for long?''

''Five years this summer.'' She stole another lick, her small pink tongue darting around the curve of the cone to catch any stray drips. ''The first two years my dad gave me a break on the rent, but since then I've been able to afford the going rate. It's a good tax write-off because I use most of it for business.''

Taxes? Business? He tried to focus on her words, but couldn't think about anything except the taxing business of resisting the urge to jump her right here, right now, on a wooden bench with a gallery of monkeys and lions voyeuristically looking on.

When he didn't respond, Amanda tugged at the front of her yellow silk blouse. ''And it's nice to have my business under my home roof. I made this tank last night for myself, and ended up creating a great pattern for my spring collection.''

Could he help it that his gaze naturally drifted to her blouse? To the tiny hint of cleavage it revealed? He scanned the landscape for a distracting exhibit. Where the hell were the warthogs when a man needed them?

''I think it's pretty impressive that you could just whip up an outfit for yourself at a moment's notice.''

''I like to play with the material,'' she admitted, waving at a gregarious tot who passed them in a stroller. ''Sometimes I forget where my hobby ends and my work begins. But I guess that's a good thing.''

''Want to know what my granddaddy used to say about all work and no play?''

She rolled her eyes. ''I bet I can guess.''

''He said I'd never have that problem.''

Her throaty laughter gave him as much fulfillment as putting crooks behind bars. A man could feel like he'd accomplished something in a day if he made Amanda Matthews laugh.

''You work very hard,'' she assured him, her gaze flicking over a strolling cotton candy vendor before returning to her cone. ''I'm sure your grandfather is very proud of you.''

Her words provided a better distraction than those warthogs. ''I hope he is. He died before I finished my training, but I'd like to think he would find a way to make his displeasure known if he wasn't proud of me. Some days when nothing goes my way I sort of get the feeling the old man is shooting thunderbolts at my butt to get me to straighten up.''

Her smile was sheepish. ''I think my mother stomps on my creativity.''

Duke thought back over the day, remembered Amanda telling him her mother had died when she was a little girl. ''Your mother meddles with you, too?''

''She's half guardian angel, half vengeful voice of my self-conscience.''

Duke reached across the bench to stroke aside a strand of her hair. The silken tress teased his skin. ''I can't imagine your mother would have too much to complain about. You're developing an ambitious career and looking out for your dad—''

The words, meant to reassure Amanda, suddenly unsettled him. He'd been able to forget about her father for most of the today. But now, thoughts of her criminally-connected family came back to remind him why he ought to be retreating instead of wondering how to get closer to her.

Ignoring all sense of caution, Duke slid a hand over hers.

Amanda stared down at their clasped hands for a long moment. ''I'd like to think so. She was a very independent woman though. Sometimes I wonder if she would think I've allowed myself to stand too much in my father's shadow."

"Not from where I'm sitting. It takes an independent woman to develop her own design business." He loosened his grip just enough to give his fingers latitude over her warm skin. With slow deliberation, he traced a path up and down her fingers, dipping lightly in between.

Was it overactive hopefulness on his part, or had she shivered?

"Work is a different story," she responded, her voice taking on a throatier note than it had a few moments ago. "Finding beauty in the ordinary is what I do best. But when it comes to my father... He's just not an easy man to confront."

Probably because he was a gangster, Duke thought, determined to keep his opinions for himself for a change. He was enjoying the day, enjoying her, far too much.

"What parents don't push their kids' buttons?"

"It's more than that." She paused as they allowed a noisy sideshow of musicians to pass. "He's got such a big personality that he sort of eclipses everyone else around him."

Duke nodded, trying to imagine anyone eclipsing the knockout beside him.

"And I'm finding it hard to make a final break from his business. Now that I'm starting to do some of my own designs, I can't really spare the time to do my father's windows, but I can't disappoint him, either. I have all the backbone of a jellyfish when it comes to my dad.''

Duke slid closer, tugging her hand into his lap and running his fingers up her inner arm. He moved slowly, not wanting to scare her off.

''You've got tons of backbone, Amanda,'' he argued, refusing to believe she couldn't stand up for herself whenever she wanted to.

Out of the corner of his eye he noticed the cone in her other hand just barely started to drip, but he didn't say anything. Yet. The small drop of chocolate ice cream slid down the cone, on a collision course with Amanda's fingers.

''I couldn't even manage to tie my own shoe after your interrogation the other day, Duke. I'm not exactly the poster child for the hip and together Millennium Woman.''

He watched the ice cream hit the fingers of her other hand and wondered what she'd do if he licked it.

Surely cleaning her off counted as being gentlemanly, didn't it?

''That didn't have anything to do with you lacking backbone,'' he assured her. Then, unable to resist, he lifted her hand, cone and all, and swirled his tongue around her fingers with the same deft thoroughness she'd used to eat her ice cream. She tasted sweet and sticky, and oh-so-right for more licking. When he finally forced himself to rein in his hunger for her, he leaned closer to whisper, ''I thought that incident with the shoe was more related to you having no clothes on.''

She pulled her hand out of his grasp, but her cheeks flushed with high color. ''How did you know?''

Hell, he'd dreamed about nothing else, night and day, since then. ''I didn't…until I saw the tape. But once I noticed the pink shoes I got the impression you were wearing the same thing in the video that you wore to Gallagher's house.''

She nodded.

He nearly groaned.

Amanda's simple acknowledgement left him harder than the damned bench. Her confirmation provided him with his best fantasy image to date—a gorgeous interrogation subject dropping her coat to reveal bare flesh and racy lingerie. Amanda might not be the poster child for the together Millennium Super-woman, but she would no doubt be the pinup queen of his sexiest dreams for the rest of his life.

''I had to have been out of my mind to make that stupid tape,'' Amanda confided.

''I thought it was a great idea,'' Duke assured her. ''Especially the last part where your outfit sort of—''

She clamped a hand over his mouth to staunch his memory of her garment sliding to the floor. ''That part was an accident.''

The palm of her hand curved around his lips while her fingers grazed his cheek. He nipped one finger with his teeth, freeing his mouth but making him hunger for another taste of her silky skin.

He wished they were at his place instead of a public park. More than anything, he wanted to explore this attraction between them, see for himself if she looked half as amazing beneath her clothes as his memory told him she did.

He shook his head. "Honey, you've got your perspective all turned around. What you're perceiving as an accident, I'm viewing as incredible good luck."

Amanda's hand tingled where Duke's teeth had scraped over her flesh. She hadn't counted on his bold move to displace her grip, but she should have. Duke didn't possess a reserved or cautious bone in his body.

And no matter how much Amanda told herself she shouldn't like it, she did.

Being around Duke was exciting. Emotionally, mentally, and—there could be no denying it—sexually.

Would she qualify as the world's most immoral woman for wanting to seduce Duke two days after she'd planned to seduce another man?

Right now, with the most charismatic man she'd ever met seated beside her, she wasn't so sure she cared.

This was different, after all. She'd never actually followed through on her plan to entice Victor, thanks to Duke. Duke had prevented her from making a mistake of monumental proportions by opening her eyes to Victor's other life. Plus, Duke had shown himself to be a gentleman by returning her secret weapon, even if he had watched it first.

She trusted him.

She wanted him.

Now all she had to do was take him home and…inspire him.

7

TWO CARAMEL APPLES, a tiger and ten llamas later, Duke and Amanda took the subway back toward the Garment District—back toward Amanda's place. Amanda had claimed she was broke except for two subway tokens and insisted on springing for transportation since Duke bought the ice cream and all the treats for her to feed the animals.

Stubborn woman.

Duke tried not to stare at her charming rear view as she made her way up the steps out of the subway.

But he wasn't that much of a gentleman.

The woman tempted him sorely even though they had next to nothing to base a relationship on. Spending the day with her hadn't done a damn thing to quench his thirst for her. If anything, he liked her even more now that he knew her better.

She wasn't just a stripteasing socialite who didn't mind breaking the rules to get what she wanted. She could haggle her way into the bargain hunter's hall of fame if she cared to. She knew the Mets' starting lineup. And she didn't just spend her time doing power lunches with her uptown friends—she had a career she cared about passionately, one that she enjoyed discussing with him. He now knew the virtues of cutting fabric on the bias, thank-you very much, and he admitted he had enjoyed studying Amanda's figure very carefully as she'd explained it to him.

Too bad none of that mattered because she was about to give him the boot and he probably wouldn't see her again until Victor's hearing.

The thought rankled all the more because he hadn't even managed to work in a kiss today. Feeding the llamas had been cool, but all he could think about now was feasting on *her*. How could he walk away from a woman like Amanda without at least a parting taste?

He noticed she'd grown quiet, too, as they approached her building. She lived over her father's studios, but the famous Clyde Matthews's showroom was dark now that it approached seven o'clock.

Duke told himself he would hand over her shopping bag and leave at any time. But he really hoped she would be receptive to a kiss first. He held no illusions that she would invite him inside, so he was a little surprised when she led him straight into her father's showroom and locked the front door behind them.

She wound her way through mannequins and rolling racks. "My loft is up here and I hate to leave the showroom unlocked for even a minute while we walk up. Do you mind coming in for a minute?" she asked over her shoulder.

She had to be kidding. Duke fought the urge to sprint. "I'm in no hurry."

Keys jingled in her hands as they journeyed up three flights of stairs. Amanda's voice drifted down as she trekked upward. "There are just a lot of locks and the door is right at the top of some stairs and—"

He hadn't realized she was nervous until the chattering started. Nervous because she wanted him here, or nervous because she needed him to go?

When he started to hear more key jingling than locks opening, Duke stepped up beside her and gently extracted the key ring from her hands. "Let me."

Her body shifted restlessly next to his. "Thank you." Her voice turned breathy in the shadowed stairwell.

They were much too close.

Her scent enveloped him, that light fragrance of a single flower. Her silk blouse shimmered softly in the dim light of the corridor, beckoning him toward her body, ensuring he could see her despite the half light.

He paused in his task, leaving the key in the last lock for just one moment while he looked at her. In the still silence that followed, her shallow breaths echoed in his ears, sending him small signals that his presence wasn't exactly unwelcome.

No matter how hard he'd tried to show her his downtown lifestyle, to reveal his simple wants in life, uptown Amanda Matthews still seemed to want *him*.

Duke hoped that sense of adventure of hers had

survived the day because he just figured out the time had arrived for that kiss.

Amanda heard the rustle of her shopping bag, saw Duke shift the sack to a step below them. She didn't think he needed both his hands free to work on that last lock to her loft.

She rather hoped he needed them to work on her.

Nerves strung tight in anticipation, Amanda didn't know what had possessed her to lead him this far into her domain. No man had ever ventured past her father's showroom to her private living space before. Even Victor had rung the bell for her downstairs and waited for her there.

Yet she'd waltzed right through the showroom and up the stairwell with Duke, unable to say good-night just yet.

He edged closer. His hands skimmed her hips, settling on her waist. Those gorgeous blue eyes glittered in the dim light, communicating his intent.

Oh yes, she wanted this.

She might have swayed right off the steps without Duke's broad palms to steady her. He guided her body to his, slanted his mouth over hers and fed her the kiss she'd hungered for all day.

The brush of his mouth electrified her, kicking her pulse into a frenzy. He tasted like caramel apples, smelled like freshly mowed grass after their afternoon at the park. His sun-warmed T-shirt grazed her silk blouse, broadcasting his body's heat to hers and making her thoughts scatter.

"Amanda." He breathed her name like an invocation, barely breaking their kiss.

"Hmm?" She stretched her arms around his shoulders, unable to open her eyes.

"Do you still have dinner plans?"

The only plan she could think of was a banquet of male muscle and Duke's kisses. "Umm...no."

"Because I wouldn't want to make you late." He leaned away a bit, inserting more space between them without untangling their arms.

That caught her attention. She forced her eyes open and found him studying her.

"You want to leave?" She had hoped to explore that kiss for just a bit longer. In fact, she seriously considered dragging the man into the loft and tossing him on the couch for a few hours while she reveled in every mind-drugging nuance of his kisses.

"No." He paused for a long moment, as if willing the word to sink in. "But if you're expecting me to walk away so you can keep your dinner engagement, then I can't afford to get trapped in a stairwell inferno." His thumb traced a slow trail over her cheek. "Which, in case you haven't noticed, is exactly what's going on here."

Amanda nodded. The sensual flames licking over her flesh confirmed his assessment. "There's no dinner engagement."

The words fell out of her mouth before she could weigh them—an impulsive sort of act she rarely com-

mitted. Her statement hung in the sultry air between
them, suggestive and vague at the same time.

Duke studied her as if she were a complex case to
solve, his keen blue gaze missing nothing. "Meaning…?"

"Meaning I'm in no rush." Had she been a more
brazen woman, she might have sidled closer to him
and shown him just what she wanted.

More fierce, hot kisses.

But since she was just Amanda Matthews, Miss
Barely Experienced, she merely waited and hoped he
understood what she wanted.

Duke looked around their close surroundings in the
darkened corridor. "Do you think maybe we should
go inside to have this discussion?"

Amanda bit her lip, unsure what to do next.

She'd enjoyed talking with Duke today, but she
didn't think she wanted to have a discussion of any
kind with him right now.

Still, maybe the stairs weren't the best place for
kissing. If she invited him in, she could fill her senses
with Duke Rawlins for a little longer, explore the
male strength of those muscles with her hands, and
then…

And then she had no idea what might happen next.

His fingers stroked over her shoulder. "I promise
not to overstay my welcome."

His touch, his gentle reassurance, prompted her to
nod. "Okay." She slid out of his arms and turned
toward the door. "It's not like it's a big deal, I've

just never had a man in my apartment before.'' She opened the last lock with the key Duke had inserted a few moments ago.

For today, at least, she would live dangerously. Duke Rawlins, bold-as-you-please detective, definitely made the perfect companion for adventure.

Duke's low whistle of appreciation pulled her from her thoughts.

He'd followed her into the loft and now stood just inside the door, gaping at the vast open space. ''Wow.''

The word echoed through the cavernous loft, bounced off the long expanses of bare hardwood floor.

Ditching her shoes, she took her shopping bags out of Duke's hands and tossed them on the floor. ''Come on in.''

He looked like he could retreat into gentleman mode at any moment and she had no patience for good behavior today. His kisses in the stairwell, his slow tasting of her fingers at the park, had her so hot and bothered she couldn't see straight.

She tugged him forward by the hand, drawing him into her world of fabric bolts and swatches. Wending around the rolling racks to her couch, Amanda drew him onto the seat beside her, wanting him close.

How bold would she have to be to get what she wanted? Didn't he know?

As she tilted her gaze up to his, she found him already staring down at her, his blue eyes searing into hers in the low light the setting sun cast over the room.

Tentatively, she reached her hand to rest on his thigh, thinking maybe a bold move would be the quickest way to inspire.

Her brain scarcely registered the low growl he made when she was scooped up and settled over his lap. His thighs cradled her bottom, providing her with an erotic seat. Her hip nudged against the hard ridge through his jeans, reassuring her it hadn't taken much effort to inspire him at all.

A surge of feminine power assailed her, making her feel more seductive than all the lingerie in the world.

Duke wanted her, too.

He cupped a hand around her neck and drew her mouth to his before she could catch her breath. His tongue stroked over hers with slow, possessive thoroughness. What little air she had left in her lungs, he somehow stole along with his kiss, as if absorbing her into him.

She threaded her fingers through his hair, wanting to feel him, needing to hang on for dear life.

Her dreams had never been this good.

She slid her palms lower to the corded muscle in his neck, the sexy ripple of his shoulders through his T-shirt. Restless for more of him, she tugged at the cotton fabric. He seemed to divine her thoughts with no effort, shrugging his way out of his shirt before pitching it to the floor.

When he came to her again, he leaned her back

into the leather cushions of her sofa, his broad chest looming above her.

The man was magnificent.

His bronze shoulders and defined abs could have leaped right off a Calvin Klein billboard. No wonder he wore a badge proclaiming, "New York's Finest."

She reached for him, desperate for his weight against her, his strength around her. But he caught her wrist before she could touch him.

"Your turn." He breathed the words in a husky rasp that sent a shiver dancing down her spine. "You think you can shimmy your way out of that blouse for me?"

He sat back on his heels as he straddled her knees, waiting, watching.

Blood pounded through her veins, making her flesh tremble with the beat of her heart. She willed her fingers to unveil herself, wanted to share this with him, but she was hypnotized by the intensity of his eyes and stricken with a sudden shyness.

His fingers came to her rescue, trailing over the hem of her shirt. "It's okay, honey, if you want to leave it on—"

"No. I want it off." She guided his fingers underneath her loose garment, fitting his palm to her waist. "I'm just not all that good at putting on a show in person, I think."

A slow smile curved his lips. His hand flexed over her hip. "By all means, allow me to help."

Amanda held her breath as the silk slid over her

flesh, baring her lace bra and plenty of skin to his gaze.

No matter how much time she put between herself and her fuller-figure days, she always feared the hips of her teenage years lurked just a few candy bars away. After spending half a lifetime struggling to cultivate a more healthy body, she was still self-conscious about her appearance.

His wolf whistle pleased her immeasurably.

He trailed a finger over her collarbone and down the slope of her breast. "Honey, you are even more mouthwatering in person." He licked the finger that had touched her, as if to prove the point.

Amanda shivered, imagining other provocative uses of his tongue. She reached for him again, wanting him too much to wait for any more undressing.

She didn't need to ask twice.

Duke covered her, blanketing her body with his own, pressing her into the creamy leather of her couch with the hard length of his body.

Her breasts beaded at the touch of his bare skin, her lace bra providing little barrier to dull her sensations.

Desire kicked through her, fueled by the gentle rasp of his lightly bristled cheek against her smooth one, his breath warm and moist near her ear.

"I don't know how I'm ever going to pry myself away from you tonight, Amanda," he whispered between kisses he trailed down her neck.

She loved it that he would walk away if she wanted

him to, that he was an honorable man despite his brash ways. "So wait until the morning," she whispered back, her whole body tensing in anticipation as he cleared her shoulder with his descending mouth.

And halted.

"Morning?" He lifted himself up on his elbows to look at her.

She longed to wriggle herself underneath him, maybe nudge the very fascinating ridge in his jeans with her thigh, anything to get him focused on her body again. But he stared down at her like spending the night was an idea he hadn't considered.

Well she had news for him.

Duke might not be the ideal man for her tomorrow or next week, but he was everything she wanted right now. She wasn't about to let him slip away.

8

"ARE YOU SURE ABOUT this, Amanda?" He had to give her one last out. One final opportunity to change her mind.

"I'm sure."

He kissed her, hard, on the mouth. "I don't have any protection with me, but I can hit a store and be back in ten minutes."

She anchored him to her. "When I went to Victor's house the other day, I was armed with my video in one pocket of my coat and a box full of protection in the other."

Bless her practicality. "You win the five-star rating tonight, Amanda Matthews."

He didn't complain when she slid out from underneath him to retrieve the box from her bathroom cabinet. He merely rolled off of her to the floor.

When she returned, he watched her move across the floor with her sexy-as-a-pinup walk. "When I first saw you going into Gallagher's building the other day, I never would have guessed you were hiding so many tantalizing secrets."

Amanda tucked the box in the couch cushions and slid to the floor beside him. "No?"

He shook his head. "Never. You've got a siren's walk, but you still put out a classy, untouchable sort of vibe."

Kneeling beside him, she trailed a finger up his arm and over his shoulder. "I hope you don't still think I'm untouchable."

In answer, he hauled her across his legs, then hooked one finger in the waistband of her skirt to sketch a path along the edge of the cotton. "I think you're ready to start revealing all those secrets you've been hiding."

Anticipation churned through Duke. The sight of Amanda's generous curves concealed by nothing but a scrap of lace was enough to make a grown man weep in appreciation. Now, he also had the enticement of her bottom settled against his thigh, her silky skin at his fingertips. When combined with the knowledge that she was his, if only for one night, Amanda Matthews set him on fire.

He bent to kiss her, scavenging for control, needing to make this right for her. Despite her bold entreaty to spend the night, Duke knew Amanda had little experience with men. Her father probably beat prospective suitors off with a stick.

So tonight had to be memorable.

"What else are you willing to show me?" he whispered between kisses, hoping the lure of their game would help slow him down, keep him from rushing to peel off her panties and seek the release his body burned for.

Her breath came in soft pants, warming his mouth, even when she wasn't receiving his kiss. ''You might have to help me with it.'' She inserted her finger in the valley between her breasts, gently tugging on the lace of her bra.

With pleasure.

His rough hands scraped over the smooth satin straps, skittered over her shoulder blades. He flicked the hook open, releasing her, spilling her lush body into his view.

What an incredible view.

Shyly, she turned into him, tucked herself and her gorgeous breasts against him. He groaned at the soft feel of her, the delicate press of her nipples into his chest.

He didn't know how much more fun and games he could take. As much as he wanted to make this night special, unforgettable, the tension ripping through him with each beat of his heart would kill him at this rate.

She rubbed her cheek on his shoulder, into his neck. She wriggled dangerously in his lap, a naively sexual ticking time bomb, ready to set him off with the slightest nudge.

Dispensing with the game, he shifted her to straddle him, his shoulders still propped against her couch. Only the city lights illuminated her loft, the dull glow from the street below filtering into the windows.

Her skirt rode up her bare thighs and Duke helped it along with eager hands. He fit her over his erection, her lace panties and his jeans still separating them and providing a frustrating as hell barrier to what he wanted.

But he wanted her to see, to feel, what she did to him.

Amanda gasped at the intimate contact. Her head tipped back, thrusting her breasts into perfect tasting position.

Duke nipped and suckled her, tasted and laved her with his tongue, drawing her into his mouth deeply. Amanda answered him with a slow ride over his lap, pressing herself into him until he thought he'd lose his mind.

He gripped her hips, stilling her while he steeled himself.

"Honey," his voice rasped thickly in the darkness. "You're killing me."

"You're not exactly being kind yourself," she whispered back with a breathy sigh. "I want to show you more."

He fought the urge to roar his gratification at her words, contenting himself to rolling her to her back, settling her into the yards of yellow silk that flowed across her floor.

She helped him free her skirt, leaving her clad in just a strip of white lace.

"I can't wait to see." He cupped her in the palm of his hand for one long moment, allowing her heat to penetrate into his skin. Amanda moaned. She shifted and writhed against him, assuring him the time was right.

Gladly, he tugged the white lace down her mile-long legs. Heaven waited for him, and all he needed to do was shuck his pants to find it.

He couldn't have stripped his clothes off faster if he'd had his own pit crew to help.

"Oh. My." Amanda looked at him with wide eyes as he stretched out over her. "You put on quite a show of your own, Detective."

"You were watching?" He pulled one corner of the yellow fabric over her shoulder, wanting to protect her silken skin from the rug.

"With rapt attention."

"Then you must know how badly I want you." He took her hand in his, guiding her to touch him.

She arched her hips beneath him in answer.

He stopped her before she could wrap her fingers around him and leaned close to her ear. "I'm going to make you want me that bad."

The feminine squeal that pierced through the room definitely made his wait worthwhile.

He kissed his way down her breasts, over her belly, to pause at the juncture of her thighs.

As much as he wanted to be inside her, he wanted the taste of her in his mouth even more. He'd barely found her sweet center, scarcely appeased his hunger for her, when her body tightened like a bow beneath him, her thighs clenching his shoulders in a vise.

He reached into the sofa cushions to retrieve her box of condoms, his hands unsteady with the need that rode him hard.

Amanda sat up, her body still shaking with aftershocks, her gaze slumberous and sexy. "Let me."

With fingers that fumbled and unwittingly teased, Amanda rolled the condom on.

Unable to linger, Duke pushed her back to their silken blanket, nudging her thighs apart with his knees. He positioned himself over her and claimed her slowly, carefully, wondering when she'd ever been with a man before and thinking how damn precious a gift she gave him.

Amanda wasn't a bored socialite attracted to his job for the excitement. She seemed to genuinely want him for him, a fact that amazed and humbled Duke.

And then she lifted her thighs to lock around his waist and he couldn't think anymore.

Every bit of his mental and physical energy was exhausted with the sheer effort not to lose himself in Amanda. Knowing he couldn't stay locked inside her legs for another minute without plummeting over the edge, he gently disengaged her feet, cupping her calves in his hands.

He eased into her again and again, nudging her to her own peak. Only when her back arched with a tension that gripped her whole body, her thighs squeezing his in a death grip, did he allow himself to hurtle over that edge with her.

A primal satisfaction poured through him long afterward, pleasure that went beyond physical to a deep sense of rightness at being there with her. Too tired, too replete to question the feeling, he merely held her in his arms.

Amanda awoke a little while later to find herself wrapped in yellow silk and Duke Rawlins. She wasn't sure if she could still move after the intense workout she'd given her body, but she knew she wanted him again.

After the incredible way he'd made her feel, she wondered if she'd ever be able to wake up and *not* want him again. The notion scared her to her pink-painted toenails.

Not that she regretted inviting Duke to stay.

No, she'd waited too long to experience this to regret their time together.

For years, she'd suspected her back seat tangle with her college beau had been less than stellar. And now she knew for certain.

She hadn't experienced anything remotely close to what Duke had introduced her to tonight. She should probably feel embarrassed that she practically screamed down the Garment District with the orgasms he gave her. But regrets and embarrassment had no place in her relationship with Duke.

Fear?

Definitely.

She had no idea where to go from here. She knew she'd have some serious thinking to do in the morning, knew that once the sun came up she'd have to figure out a plan for how to deal with all of this.

But for right now, she only wanted to think about

how to move a six-foot rock of a man from her living room floor to her bed.

Wrapping herself in the remaining length of yellow silk, Amanda suspected enticement was her best option.

She happened to know Duke was rather fond of show-and-tell, and she planned to show him she still had plenty of secrets to reveal.

SEVEN HOURS AND three condom packages later, Amanda knew she wouldn't be able to move. She didn't care how much it turned her on to see Duke's broad shoulders sprawled across her bed, she had to ignore him if she ever wanted to start her day and finish her designs.

She needed to get to work after taking the entire previous day off. She spent so much time helping her father during the week the only way she'd been able to start her own company had been to work nights and weekends on her own projects.

Amanda slid straight from the bed into her robe, more self-conscious of her body in the light, even though Duke still slept. She definitely wasn't ready for him to see her without her glamorous exterior in place. Although she didn't need much makeup, she did work hard to look pulled together, to have her hair stylized, her eyes enhanced by whatever the newest trend in cosmetics happened to be.

Her father appreciated beauty around him at all times, and Amanda had learned long ago she fit in to his world more easily when she complied. Even now, on a day when she wouldn't be seeing her father, she found herself carefully constructing the façade the rest of the fashion world acquainted with her signature style.

By the time she'd showered and dressed in working clothes—a slim skirt and a crisp men's dress shirt—Amanda could smell breakfast cooking.

Her belly growled in response even as she worried about facing him again. She'd never done this before, never had to face any man on the morning after. How did one behave?

"Hey, gorgeous," Duke called easily from his place at the stove. "Who's Lexi?"

She blinked, taking in his brawny body at home in her tiny kitchen, his deft flipping of pancakes in a frying pan she didn't know she possessed, his question....

"Lexi?" she parroted, drawn forward by the aroma.

Duke picked up a carton of eggs and read off of a purple sticky note attached to it. "It says, 'Girlfriend, you have the most atrociously stocked fridge of any woman I know. I brought you some eggs, but save me two for the dinner I'm making you on Wednesday.'" Duke moved a bottle of pancake syrup to Amanda's kitchen table. "Is this Lexi any competition I need to worry about or anything? Is that some kind of Russian name?"

His blue eyes were mischievous, but he watched her intently while waiting for her answer.

Amanda moved into the kitchen and pulled down the juice glasses. "No. It's short for Alexandra. Lexi is my best friend."

Duke flipped the last batch of pancakes out of the pan and onto a plate already stacked high. "Excellent. So I don't have to worry about any big Russian guy showing up at your door and fighting me for you?"

The image brought a smile to her face. "Hardly. Although if you were to get on Lexi's bad side for some reason, my money is always on her in a fight."

Duke put their plates on the table and held out her chair. "You wound me, Amanda. I'm tougher than I look, you know."

Amanda didn't imagine many other detectives boasted such a strong physique, but she didn't think Duke needed any help with his self-image. She helped herself to a taste of her breakfast, starving after the most athletic night of her life. "Lexi is the champion of lost causes and she can wrest money from the stingiest skinflint on the Upper East Side. She's pretty tough."

And even though she'd never stood higher than Amanda's shoulder, Lexi had always been able to scare off any boarding school bully that crossed her path.

"You've obviously forgotten you're talking to one of New York's Finest."

Amanda reached for the butter. She didn't want to

insult Duke, but the pancakes tasted like health food, probably because he'd made them with the only kind of flour Lexi ever stocked—wheat flour. "I haven't forgotten." She smiled at him to ensure he wasn't offended that she was using more butter. "In fact, I think it's pretty exciting. My family's reputation has been cast into question my whole life, thanks to my father's friendships with disreputable people. It's neat to hang around with a guy who's sort of above reproach." She rambled as she reached for the syrup.

Duke observed her closely. Had he noticed her second round of syrup?

"So you were attracted by the whole cop thing?"

Amanda shrugged, wondering if it would be worse to have him realize she thought his pancakes were a little dry or to have him think she was a couple of months away from her fuller-figure clothes. She nudged the syrup away again. "Well sure, who wouldn't be? Your job must be nonstop action and adventure."

He watched her with sort of an odd disillusionment scrawled across his features. Amanda swore he was seeing straight through her carefully cultivated façade.

Nervous, she rambled more. "Besides, cops are sort of safe dates, aren't they? A sense of honor comes with the territory. I mean, a badge is like a seal of approval. Or maybe a five-star rating in your case."

Duke finished his last bite and wasted no time pushing to his feet and clearing his plate.

Amanda knew she'd somehow gained back twenty pounds over breakfast because he didn't even seem to see her anymore.

"Glad I could show you a good time, Amanda. I probably need to let you move on with your day while I return to my adventures on the police force." He cleared her plate for her, too, even though she hadn't finished her pancakes.

She stood, mute, while he rinsed the dishes and put them in the dishwasher. What had she done to warrant this brusque behavior? And who was this terse stranger hustling around her kitchen?

Amanda gathered her scrambled thoughts just as he finished wiping down her stovetop. "I'm sorry if I'm not very good at this." She took a stab in the dark, not sure if he was upset with her or if this was just how mornings-after proceeded. So far, she definitely did not like them. "I just haven't really done this before."

For a moment, his serious expression softened. She thought she glimpsed a hint of the man she'd known yesterday.

"That's okay." He crossed the kitchen and paused in front of her.

Her every nerve ending leapt at his proximity.

Apparently, his nerve endings weren't half so inspired, because he leaned down to brush a kiss across her forehead. "I've got to get back to work, Amanda. I'll call you to let you know when Gallagher's hearing is scheduled.'' His gaze narrowed. ''You will still testify, won't you?''

Amanda had never been given such a heartless dismissal in her whole life. Some of that had to do with the fact that she'd never let a man get close enough to hurt her so much as Duke did in that moment. But the majority of blame she placed squarely on Duke's broad shoulders.

''I am happy to wreak my vengeance on people who treat me abominably,'' she tossed back, even though it wasn't true. She hurt inside and she didn't have a clue what to do about it. She hadn't wanted a man in her life on a steady basis right now, but she hadn't meant to send Duke running in the other direction, either.

At least not yet.

Duke retrieved his wallet from her living room end table, working his way toward the door.

She walked him out, her sense of etiquette demanding she be polite even though he seemed to have forsaken all his good manners now that he had slept with her.

As she unlocked the showroom door, she couldn't help but think how different her mood had been when they'd entered that door yesterday.

''Bye, Duke.'' She wasn't good at playing haughty, and she really hated the note they were ending on. Maybe that's why she found herself saying, ''I had a good time yesterday.''

He paused, lingering longer than she'd expected.

Their gazes met, locked.

"You'd better go," she prompted. "I bet you're pretty dazzling out there, saving the world."

She'd meant to flatter him, to end on a light note. Besides, she *did* see his job as noble and honorable.

Too bad he visibly shut down at her words, his gaze sliding away from hers.

"That's me—superhero of the streets." He flashed her a cocky grin that lacked his usual warmth, then planted a formal kiss on her cheek before propelling his way through the door.

As Amanda watched him through the showroom window, she refused to feel guilty or ashamed of her actions. She'd obviously just misjudged Duke.

Either that or he'd gotten a peek behind her carefully cultivated façade and didn't admire the woman she really was.

In which case, she shouldn't want him anyway.

Trudging back up the stairs to her loft, Amanda vowed she wouldn't allow her one attempt at adventure to taint her workday. She had a job to do—several in fact—to prepare for her fall shows and she wasn't about to retreat into a tub of ice cream to soothe her raw emotions.

She hadn't created a splash in the designer community with that kind of attitude.

Still, she couldn't help thinking if Lexi hadn't stocked her cupboards with her health nut food and wheat flour, Amanda might now be tearing open yet another condom packet with her teeth.

9

SHOVING THROUGH THE back door of the fifth design house on his list of prospects, Duke emerged onto Eighth Avenue frustrated and impatient.

Over a week had passed since Gallagher's arrest, but drugs still poured through the Garment District. The special task force that Duke and his partner were assigned to had stepped up their efforts to address the problem, but Duke had been striking out all morning.

Rather, it seemed he'd been striking out ever since he'd walked out of Amanda's loft five days ago.

Damn.

The woman had practically admitted to going out with him simply because he was a cop, that she equated his job with adventure. Didn't he know better than to tread down that path again?

Still, he found himself feeling like he'd been the jerk in the long run, not calling her the day after their…night. God knows, he'd been thinking about her. As he walked south a couple of blocks, hoping to run into Josh, Duke wondered if Amanda had been thinking about him.

He'd been thinking about her pretty much nonstop.

His first mistake had been bringing his backup copy

of her steamy video to his house. He'd told himself he wasn't going to do anything other than put it some place safe from all possibility of prying eyes. But by the next day, his eyes were the ones longing to pry. For two days, he'd stalked past that damn tape in his living room, cursing and blessing it at the same time.

The videotape proved to have as much allure as the woman, tempting him to the limits of reason, past the boundaries of his ethics, and straight to his VCR. Once he'd given in to his half-obsessed desire to see her again, he'd been utterly absorbed by her show, reveling in every nuance of her sexy unveiling, enrapt by the way she slid out of her clothes to offer herself to the viewer.

Now, the well-memorized images of that videotape seemed to replay in one tantalizing loop in his mind.

He had to admit, Amanda Matthews kept him pretty damn distracted.

A low whistle from his right halted his steps and his mental video replay.

Duke turned to see Josh emerging from another design house.

"Don't tell me you're daydreaming again, Rawlins." Josh scowled. "Did you even remember we were supposed to meet?"

With Amanda on the brain, what red-blooded guy would be able to think of anything else? "I've got bad guys to catch, Winger. I can't wait around for you all day." Duke drew up his shoulders and hitched at the lapels to his jacket. "You think the Terminator would wait around for Columbo?"

Josh fell into step with him as they trekked south through the Garment District. "If he had any sense he would. Didn't your granddaddy ever tell you the one about the tortoise and the hare?"

Only about a million times. "Never heard that one. Granddaddy was more of the mind that nice guys finish last. You find anything out, Columbo?"

Josh jerked his thumb toward Thirty-sixth Street. "Let's head this way."

Duke steeled himself for a walk by Clyde Matthews's showroom. Amanda's loft. Didn't matter to him, right? He was focused on his investigation, *not* the way he'd mishandled the other morning with Amanda. He'd probably overreacted.

He'd been meaning to call Amanda to at least say hello, to apologize for the abrupt way he'd left. He'd sent her flowers the next day, but he still didn't know what to say about their night together.

Josh pulled out a piece of paper from his pants' pocket.

"Herb Rainey." He shoved the paper back in his pocket. "That's the name of the guy who took Gallagher's place as fabric supplier to that last designer. Why don't we stop by Matthews's and see if they know this guy? Could be he's taking over Gallagher's importation scheme."

And see Amanda? Not that Duke couldn't manage a routine questioning with the most distracting woman in Manhattan. Still, he couldn't help but come up with alternatives.

"Why don't we just run this guy's name through customs and see what we come up with?" He pulled out his cell phone to conduct the request immediately.

Not that he was avoiding the curvaceous temptation of Miss High Society who liked to walk on the wild side.

Josh yanked the phone out of his hand. "What's the matter, Rawlins? Scared you might run into the mob princess?"

Duke grit his teeth. Cop politics weren't that much different from playground politics, and he sure as hell couldn't let his buddies call him chicken.

"Amanda Matthews isn't exactly hard on the eyes. Why would I mind seeing her?" Duke wrenched his phone out of Josh's grip. "But being a hare as opposed to a damn tortoise, I don't particularly like to waste time. It'll be quicker to see what customs knows."

"You *are* running scared." Josh shook his head. "What happened that day you took her out? Did she sic her old man on you?"

"You think the Terminator couldn't handle the mob?" Duke hissed, waiting for the call he'd placed to go through. "What was that fabric guy's name again?"

"Rainey."

They shuffled around the street corner while Duke

relayed the information to a customs agent who was part of their special task force.

As Duke hung up the phone, Josh looked at him expectantly. "Anything?"

"He can't get back to us until five o'clock. He's out on the street." Duke knew what that meant, but he didn't like it.

"So we might as well talk to Matthews or his daughter as long as we're down here." Josh slugged Duke's arm. "Don't worry, Romeo, I'll do the talking for you."

"You're pushing it, Winger." Anticipation punched through him at the thought of seeing her again, and that's exactly what he had hoped to avoid.

Damn.

Before Duke could light into a much-needed argument with Josh, a uniformed officer emerged from a coffee shop, distracting them for a moment.

While Josh high-fived the beat cop, Duke took deep breaths in a last-ditch effort to get his head on straight.

When Josh turned his attention back to Duke, he picked up right where they'd left off.

"Just trying to figure out why you could barely peel yourself off her that day at the precinct and ever since you took her out you've been hangdogging it big-time. What gives?"

"Nothing. There is nothing going on between me and Amanda Matthews." And it was going to stay that way.

She'd obviously had her fun, and next time she

went looking for adventure, she'd probably find another cop to show her a good time.

The image socked him in the gut. What was he thinking?

On second thought, he'd definitely be willing to sacrifice himself to her curiosity again if she was ever interested. He wouldn't want anyone else seeing what he'd seen the other night.

Josh sighed. "Fine. Nothing is going on. But I hope you didn't piss her off so much she won't testify for you. You know that upgrade of yours is contingent on convictions not arrests, right? Any poor clod can arrest people. Only the cops with the best investigative skills—and cooperative witnesses—can make convictions."

Duke swiped his hand across his forehead, not that he was starting to sweat this, but it sure was hot for May.

They'd just arrived at the Matthews's showroom and he had to admit Josh had a good point. He needed Amanda's help and it wouldn't pay to ruffle her feathers.

Normally, he found it easy to play the good cop to Josh's bad cop. Charming had always come easily to him. But he had the feeling he'd be hard-pressed to make the grade today when all he could think about was how it had felt to sleep with Amanda plastered to him all night long.

He needed Gallagher's conviction.

Badly.

What if Amanda was upset he hadn't called her? Would she refuse to testify just to spite him? She'd probably been going against her father's wishes to testify in the first place. Maybe she'd be more than happy to follow his orders now that she had no reason to do Duke any favors.

He scraped a hand through his hair in a vain hope to stimulate his brain. He'd been thinking with his pants, and—of all stupid things—his heart. But now he needed to get serious. He had a job to do and he would make sure Amanda showed up for her court appointment, even if it took major groveling.

He hadn't meant to hurt her. He just hadn't known what to say to her once he knew she'd only been out for fun.

Why had he hoped she might have wanted more?

Duke nodded to his partner, conveying the go-ahead to proceed. "We're going in. I'm doing the talking, so you just do what you do best."

Josh grinned. "Keep my mouth shut and look scary?"

"Don't get too high on yourself there, Columbo." Duke pulled the door open and stepped into the Clyde Matthews showroom.

He could handle this.

Too bad he felt less like the Terminator and more like one of the Hardy Boys when he spotted her kneeling in the front of the store and leaning into the display window.

Her bottom wriggled invitingly, making his mouth

go dry, his blood run hot and his heart beat a tango rhythm against his chest. Memories of her video assailed him, the way she sauntered around her private runway in fuchsia silk, her siren's walk all the more devastating because she was half-naked....

His condition downgraded to one of the Hardy Boys watching his first skin flick and was rapidly deteriorating.

Amanda heard the bell ring on the showroom door, but she couldn't get one of the mannequin's shoes on her plastic foot. Why did they make these display mannequins' extremities so small? No real woman could walk around without falling on such little feet.

Amanda knew the clerk at the counter could help the customer who'd just walked in. In the meantime, she was determined to make the size five shoe work, even if she had to staple the leather to the synthetic model.

At least she was determined until she heard the masculine throat clearing close behind her.

An innocuous enough sound, right?

Could be anyone in the world standing behind her clearing their throat, but the sudden stinging awareness jolting through her suggested the newcomer wasn't just anyone. No. The hot stirring in her veins suggested the newcomer was a very particular someone.

"Hello, Amanda." Duke Rawlins's seductive voice seemed to suggest long, languorous lovemaking and scintillating morning quickies even if he was talking about the weather.

Maybe that's why steam seemed to hiss from her whenever he got close.

But she had to remember he wasn't interested in her on a long-term basis any more than she was interested in him. In fact, he'd somehow seen through her hard-won glamorous shell to the person inside and had taken off at a dead run. So she determined she would be an ice princess today at all costs, no matter how charming the flashy detective played it.

Reluctantly, she backed out of the window and stood. "Hello, Detective." She noticed a tall, intimidating-looking man behind Duke. The scar on his face, the forbidding expression, made her wonder if Duke had toted his latest arrest into the showroom.

"This is my partner, Detective Josh Winger." He jerked his thumb toward the man who bore more resemblance to one of her father's associates than a New York cop.

"Pleased to meet you." Amanda extended her hand, drawing on her boarding school manners to get her through an awkward situation.

"Same here." Detective Winger shook her hand, then pointed toward the back of the shop. "Mind if I have a look around while you two…talk?"

"Not at all." Although now she'd be all the more alone with Duke, and given the peculiar way her heart currently raced, she really wished the criminal-looking detective would come back.

She watched Duke's tall partner duck under mannequins' arms and poke at sequined dresses until Duke's hand grazed her arm and brought all her focus crashing into that small patch of skin where he'd touched her.

His eyes skated over her, thawing her ice princess veneer way too quickly.

"I'm sorry I didn't get in touch with you earlier this week."

She stiffened, recalling exactly why she needed to be frosty. "Thank you for the flowers. I'm sure that was sufficient." They had been daisies and some other wildflowers she didn't recognize, which seemed marginally more thoughtful than roses. But when Duke's call never came, she began to view the flowers as a gesture to assuage his guilt rather than a token of any affection.

Wincing, he scrubbed a restless hand over his tie, which was decorated with comets, planets, a green Martian and—surprise, surprise—lots of stars. "I'd like to be more than sufficient for you, Amanda."

Was it her imagination or did he look as shocked by his own words as she was?

"You did an admirable job of hiding that fact." She glanced over at Duke's partner, who seemed to be absorbed in figuring out how to pose one of the mannequins on the floor. He carefully positioned the plastic model's head to the right, then to the left.

Turning her attention back to Duke, she couldn't resist speaking her mind. "And excuse me if I find it hard to believe that you genuinely came here to talk to me about what happened between us when you arrive with your Rottweiler partner, ready to nose around my father's business.'' She made a sweeping gesture with her arm. "Have at it, Duke. You hardly need my permission to search the place.''

Duke levered her extended arm back to her side. "That's not my intent.''

He watched her gaze narrow and braced himself for her next accusation. He had walked in here expecting a cool reception, but he hadn't been expecting to see hurt in her eyes.

Had he been wrong about her motives the other night?

Amanda crossed her arms over her chest, a defensive gesture on anyone else, a provocative as hell move on her, considering the lush breasts she cinched her arms around. The crisp linen of her jacket molded to her curves, outlining a view that sent his blood rushing south.

"What exactly is your intent, Duke?''

She did *not* want to know the answer to that one. Not at this moment.

Her impatient sigh distracted him from his way-too-lustful thoughts.

"I did stop by to ask you a question about the investigation, Amanda.'' He owed it to her to be honest, but the stiffening of her shoulders didn't make it easy.

Before she could tell him off, he brushed his fingers

down her arm, unable to keep his hands to himself around her. "I screwed up last weekend and I know that. Things happened so fast between us that I wasn't really prepared for how to deal with it. That night with you rocked the damn earth for me, Amanda. I guess I just needed to back up for a few days to get my head on straight again."

She seemed to be weighing his explanation, deciding whether or not he was feeding her a line.

The kicker of it all was that the words falling out of his mouth now made more sense than any of the crap he'd been telling himself all week.

"I mean, you have to admit, the other night was phenomenal."

She lifted a skeptical brow.

"Not that I'm trying to take all the credit for it." He peered around the store to make sure no one else lurked within earshot of their conversation. "You were pretty amazing yourself."

The blush on her cheeks suggested she remembered that night as thoroughly as he did.

"Apparently it didn't matter to you how amazing it might have been," she finally returned, each word annunciated with crisp precision. "You still decided to put me on ice in the morning and then walk out the door without looking back."

Duke scrambled for the words to make things right between them, the approach that would melt her just a little. "I made you breakfast at least."

He thought he saw one corner of her mouth quirk.

"Wheat pancakes are a poor excuse for a morning-after breakfast."

"You're not a health nut I take it?"

"The wheat flour is something Lexi must have bought."

"Next time I'll go out for strawberries and chocolate." He should have realized a woman who could appreciate the decadence of a triple dip ice-cream cone probably wouldn't be overly enthused about wheat pancakes for breakfast.

"There obviously won't ever be a next time for us, but perhaps your next conquest would appreciate the gesture." She stepped away from him, back toward the window she'd been designing when he'd arrived. "Now if you'll excuse me, I really need to get back to work."

He was striking out swinging here, and the sick feeling in his gut didn't have anything to do with his case or Amanda's testimony. He wanted another chance with her, another night to understand her for who she really was instead of viewing her through the bad experience he'd had with uptown types in the past. "Can I see you this weekend?"

She was going to shoot him down, he could tell by her expression.

But he was saved from the blow by the showroom door crashing open. While the store welcome bell rang over and over again, a tall man dressed in a black T-shirt and perfectly creased pants stood framed in the entrance.

"Bonjour!" he shouted, flinging his arms wide as if he expected the world to come running to him.

Surprisingly, it did.

Amanda hurried over to greet the man and so did the store clerk. Amanda kissed his cheek while the clerk kissed the air alongside his other cheek.

A third woman wearing tiny silver-rimmed glasses scurried in behind the newcomer, a leather ledger under one arm. She ignored the kissing group and carefully placed her ledger under the front desk and then started shuffling papers on the countertop.

"Good morning, Daddy," Amanda murmured, brushing a stray piece of lint from the older man's shoulder.

This was her father?

Duke had seen photos of Clyde Matthews somewhere, but the pictures of the distinguished-looking, gray-haired gentleman hadn't prepared him for someone so boisterous. The guy strutted around the showroom like a rooster in a henhouse, or maybe a successful artist in his garret. His voice booming as he recounted an anecdote from his morning, Matthews's cup of coffee flailed through the air while he talked with his hands. Each swipe of his arm brought the beverage perilously close to the edge of the foam cup.

The woman who'd entered behind Clyde Matthews tore off several paper towels from a roll on the front counter, as if she'd seen him in action before.

"We have guests, I see." He smiled broadly at

both Duke and Josh as he finished his tale. "Welcome, friends."

Duke hoped the guy didn't expect *him* to come running, too. He acknowledged the man with a nod.

"Can I help you gentlemen find anything?" Clyde Matthews's eyes traveled over Duke's clothes, pausing on the necktie. "I've got everything a welldressed man would appreciate."

Duke wondered if Amanda's father suggested he didn't have a damn thing for guys like him and his partner, but he kept his response to a minimum. "No thanks. We just stopped to ask a couple of questions."

Matthews looked vaguely annoyed. But instead of turning his frown to his "guests," Matthews scowled in his daughter's direction. "Amanda?"

Duke felt his hackles rise. Even more so when Amanda half-jumped into action.

"They are New York police detectives, Daddy," she supplied smoothly, her voice quiet and soothing next to Matthews's booming, expressive one. "I believe they are following up on Victor Gallagher's arrest."

"A pity about Victor," her father noted.

Duke felt Josh's presence stealing across the showroom floor like the imposing shadow he was. Josh never said much when they went someplace together, falling into his tough guy guise with ease and—Duke was pretty certain—pleasure.

"Actually, the New York Police Department is

very pleased to have Gallagher behind bars,'' Duke corrected the designer as Josh moved silently into place behind him. ''We would like to know if anyone has offered to take Gallagher's place as one of your fabric suppliers this week.''

Matthews's eyes darted over Josh. ''No one has presented themselves yet.''

Amanda leaned forward into the polite male face-off, gently touching her father's arm. ''You must have forgotten, Daddy. A man left his card for you just yesterday.''

Matthews set his coffee on the front counter with a slam, splashing the brew all over the bespectacled woman's papers. ''Whose side are you on, Amanda? They carted off your boyfriend last week and now they want to lock up every fabric supplier in the city. And you want to help them?''

Amanda frowned, clearly annoyed, yet her voice remained as smoothly placating as before. ''Victor was a criminal, Daddy. And he might have criminal friends taking his place. We don't want to do business with them.''

Matthews picked up his coffee again, seemingly oblivious to the woman scrambling around behind him with paper towels to clean up his spills. The silent ledger-carrier scowled so hard her glasses were skewed on her nose.

''I like doing business with people who are respect-ful.'' Matthews glared at Duke, almost as if he'd picked up something going on between him and Amanda on his parental radar.

Unless Amanda had told him what happened.

Duke gulped. Matthews didn't intimidate him a bit, but Duke couldn't help but feel guilty for the way he'd treated Amanda. He didn't need her father's censuring look to remind him he'd screwed up.

Amanda sighed. "Of course Victor was respectful. Thanks to your business as a convenient cover-up, he was able to smuggle drugs into the city and make a mint."

"At least he knew how to dress." Matthews smiled like an unrepentant child. "Will you get me my sketchpad, sweetheart, so I can go to work? I had the best ideas this morning at the coffee shop. I need to get them on paper before I lose them."

The designer stalked into the back room with his sloshing cup in hand, singing an aria at the top of his lungs.

Amanda nodded to the clerk who jumped to follow the man, a sketchpad in her hands.

"Sorry about that." Amanda offered Duke a tight smile. "My father resides in an artistic world that doesn't always overlap the real one. The man who offered his services yesterday was named Henry. No, Herbert." She nodded, sure of her facts. "Herbert Rainey."

Josh pulled out his cell phone and started dialing before the words were all out of her mouth.

Duke took the opportunity to drape his arm around

her shoulders, to touch her for another minute. "Thanks, Amanda. I appreciate you helping me with this case."

She ducked out of his grasp, but her simple fragrance lingered in his mind, firing up his senses with memories of their night together. "Despite my father's attitude, I assure you our business is police-friendly and we are happy to help in any way we can."

"Does that mean you will still testify against Gallagher?"

She blew a stray hair off her face with a twisted gesture of her mouth, an act that both aroused the hell out of him and made him wonder if uptown Amanda hid a down-to-earth side somewhere under that sleek veneer of hers.

"Of course I will testify. I promised I would, didn't I?"

Yeah, but Duke had been too busy telling himself she was probably as shallow as other women he'd known in his life to believe her.

Because the bespectacled woman at the counter still watched their actions with interest, Duke kept his response to a minimal brush of his hand across Amanda's cheek. A too-brief stroke of her hair behind one ear. "Thank you, Amanda."

He knew the feel of her cool skin, the scent of her soft hair, would torment him all day. He looked forward to it.

Even more, he looked forward to finding a way to

win her back and finagle his way into her good graces again. Maybe all his granddad's lessons about how to be a charming gentleman instead of a brazen scapegrace would finally find a practical application.

She straightened, but Duke could see the light flush in her cheeks, the quick way she breathed in the rapid rise and fall of her chest.

Oh yes. This was one mistake he would be only too happy to correct. He'd correct his other mistake— keeping the backup copy of her videotape—after Gallagher's hearing when he could confess he'd kept it and then hand it over to her. For now, all he could think about was getting her alone with a bolt of silk and those high-heel shoes of hers....

He steeled himself for another day of being driven to distraction by sizzling memories of Amanda. He just hoped the fireworks between them wouldn't blow up in his face.

10

Her skin still tingling where Duke's touch had lingered, Amanda watched him back toward the front door of the showroom.

The spell seemed to have finally broken for her father's nosy bookkeeper, Karen Wells, now that Duke was leaving the showroom. The woman had scarcely taken her eyes off him from the moment she'd walked in with her ever-present ledger.

Amanda didn't know what had made Duke warm up to her again, but she knew she shouldn't be experiencing hot fantasies about a guy whose affections were about as reliable as New York public transportation.

Been there. Done that. Ditched the fickle almost-fiancé.

"Bye, Duke." She offered what she hoped was a polite, professional smile, then called to his partner still connected to his cell phone, "Nice meeting you, Detective Winger."

The tall detective nodded his acknowledgement as he opened the front door.

And promptly entangled himself and Duke in a traffic jam.

"Well *hello*," a familiar Long Island accent drifted from amidst the big male bodies in the entry. "Is there a sale on sunglasses that I don't know about?"

Lexi emerged from the wall of muscle, her poodle in her arms and a flirtatious grin painted in stop-traffic red across her face. "Your clientele is improving, Amanda," she commented loud enough for the departing detectives to hear. "I like it."

Duke was already out the door, but Amanda noticed Josh Winger stood in the entrance a little longer, his eyes plastered to Lexi's body-hugging blue crocheted dress.

Only when Lexi turned and waved her poodle's paw at the detective did the man seem to remember himself. With a curt nod he let go of the door and disappeared into the pedestrian traffic of the Garment District.

Lexi whistled as she set her dog on the floor. "Girl, that gorgeous manflesh nearly made me forget what I came for. Muffin, you sit right there." She helped herself to a side table with gourmet coffee and pastries. "They were cops, right?"

Amanda nodded. She reached under the counter to find her own mug. "Yes. They were investigating Victor Gallagher."

"Those were the guys? Which one was Duke?"

"The blond with the solar system on his tie."

"And you didn't introduce me?" Lexi stamped both her feet on the Italian marble floor. "How could you let them just stroll away like that?"

Amanda shrugged. "Sorry. But I've barely forgiven Duke Rawlins for giving me the coldest shoulder of my life. Besides, they didn't exactly come for a social visit."

"That reminds me." Lexi sipped her coffee. "Neither did I. But first, did Duke abjectly apologize for beating tracks from your door last weekend?"

Amanda hadn't meant to tell Lexi about what had happened with Duke, but her friend's shrewd eye had observed Amanda's less-than-jubilant mood this week and she'd been relentless about unearthing the cause. Amanda had ended up giving her a pared down version of her parting of the ways with the flashy detective.

"He apologized," Amanda admitted. "But that doesn't mean...well I don't know what it means, but I'm not seeing him again."

Lexi waggled her eyebrows. "Except at Victor's hearing."

"A very public venue where there will be lots of other people." Amanda did not want to think about seeing Duke again. Not when he'd walked out with that charm-your-socks-off grin on his face. She knew she was toast if he turned his skills to charming her. "Now, what brings you to the showroom?"

Lexi grabbed Amanda by the arm for an answer, tugging her toward the front door.

Amanda stumbled along behind her, her freshly poured hazelnut breakfast blend sloshing around her cup as badly as her father's normally did.

"I wanted to see what you're doing with your window this week." Lexi dragged her through the front door to stand on the street right in front of Amanda's latest display. Muffin followed, his nails scraping the concrete.

They stood in the bright May sunshine, studying her vignette. Amanda still saw the flaws, the imperfections she hadn't yet fixed, but Lexi was already raving.

"It's fabulous." She squeezed Amanda's arm as if to offer a silent congratulations. "The daisy in the teeth is great."

Inspired by her trip to Canal Street, Amanda had posed her mannequins in a setting to evoke the market atmosphere. The main female mannequin danced to a street vendor's guitar music, a daisy in her teeth and a skirt of yellow silk swirling around her legs thanks to a small electric fan Amanda had hidden. The male mannequin watched in the background, his arms full of shopping bags.

"That skirt isn't a Clyde Matthews though," Lexi observed right away. "Is it yours?"

"It is now. I just thought of it while I worked on the window." The yellow silk had been very inspiring thanks to memories of sliding around in it with Duke.

"You're putting your own designs in a Clyde Matthews window?" She sounded scandalized.

"The man won't listen to me when I tell him I don't have time to do his displays anymore." She nudged Lexi forward, out of the way of a skateboarder careening down the sidewalk. "I figure if I'm going to invest the time, I might as well reap some benefit." The move had been underhanded, maybe, but Amanda had suffered her father's manipulative tactics for getting his own way for long enough.

Lexi shook her head. "Everyone is going to go ballistic over that skirt. It's the best thing in the window."

Amanda couldn't help but smile. She'd thought it was pretty good as she'd created it, but her friend's expert assurance as one of New York's most respected fashion reviewers bolstered Amanda's confidence. "Thank you."

"Your father's going to kill you when his next twenty customers want that skirt. Your skirt."

Amanda hoped not. It hadn't been her intention to upset her father. "No. But maybe he'll finally get his head out of the clouds and acknowledge me as a fellow designer instead of his personal assistant and daughter. I've tried to talk to him, Lex, but every conversation just ends up with him singing another aria."

Lexi nodded, snapping her fingers for Muffin as she edged toward the showroom door. "Hey, you won't hear me arguing. You need to make him notice you."

Amanda followed Lexi into the store, stealing a soothing sip of the hazelnut brew to banish thoughts of her father.

"So did your cop look at your window?" Lexi

asked, dropping onto the antique sofa near the show-room's lone posh dressing room.

In a flash, Amanda's thoughts of her father were obscured by visions of Duke Rawlins. Had he noticed the Canal Street vignette on his way out? Heaven knew, those scorching blue eyes didn't miss much. And the male mannequin was Duke, right down to his starry tie. "I don't think so."

"But he did come here to kiss your toes for not calling this week, right?"

Amanda seated herself across on a carpeted plat-form in front of a three-way mirror. "He said he freaked because of how fast things went between us."

Lexi leaned forward in her seat. Muffin sat up at her feet in perfect imitation. "Really?" She tapped the rim of her cup with one long, two-tone blue-painted fingernail. "Where did you say Duke is from? New York?"

Amanda shrugged. "I'm not sure. Why?"

"I'm just trying to figure out what kind of guy he is, what his intentions might be."

Standing, Amanda brushed off her narrow skirt, im-patient to end all talk of Duke. "You're not my psy-chic hotline advisor, Lex. I don't need you to figure out his intentions for me."

"How old is he?" Lexi pressed.

Thirty-ish? "I don't know."

Lexi rolled her eyes. "Geesh, Amanda. You spent a whole day and night with him. What did you guys talk about? Do you know what he likes to do besides hunt down bad guys? Or if Duke is even his real name?"

"He likes the Mets," Amanda ventured, wishing she could come up with enough to hush Lexi before her friend launched into a tirade about intelligent dating.

What *had* she and Duke talked about when they'd spent the day together? Amanda recalled Duke listening attentively while she explained the difference between crepes and silks and silk georgette. She remembered pointing out hemlines on women all over the city and his interest in bias-cut fabric.

God, she must have bored the poor man to tears.

"All cops like baseball." Lexi shook her head. "I can't believe you, of all people, slept with a guy you barely knew." She shot Amanda a wicked grin. "He must have really knocked your stockings off."

To put it mildly, yes.

As she led Lexi upstairs to her loft, Amanda tried not to think about how much Duke Rawlins had shook up her world in the course of a few days.

And remembering the way he'd touched her before he left the showroom today, Amanda had the feeling he was going to try it again. Soon.

This time she'd be ready for him.

This time she knew how charming he could be and she wouldn't let him "knock her stockings off."

Amanda fanned herself at the mere thought.

As memories of their night together flooded back

in a heated crush, somehow she didn't think she'd ever be able to strap on her garters tight enough.

DUKE STARED DOWN at the desk calendar beside his computer at the precinct, surprised to realize it had only been two weeks since he'd renewed his efforts to woo Amanda.

Why then, did it seem like a lifetime?

Two weeks and she was still avoiding him—hiding out in her loft when he visited the showroom and refusing his offers to take her out. How could he apply the "Good Cop" charm when she wouldn't even let him get anywhere near her?

Today, at Victor Gallagher's hearing, she would have no choice.

Josh's voice called from behind. "Hey Duke, you up for poker tonight at the chief's place?"

Turning, Duke shook his head. "No thanks. My luck has dried up this month, I think."

"No kidding." Josh plunked down into his own chair a few desks away. "Why else would we invite you?"

Duke laughed despite the slight gnawing in his gut at the notion of his luck fading. He'd always been able to charm his way through life. The thought that he'd really blown his chance with Amanda was bad enough in itself. He couldn't stand the idea of going through life with only a video version of Amanda—as tantalizing as that version might be. What if his luck on the job vanished, too? Not a good thought for a cop. "Maybe next week."

"You need me at Gallagher's hearing?"

Duke plucked up the stress ball and squeezed it. "Nope. I've got enough to hold him."

"Assuming the mob princess shows up."

He ground his teeth. "Leave it be, Winger. She's going to come through."

Amanda didn't want anything more to do with Duke, but he believed her when she said she'd testify. Her father might foster underworld connections, but Duke was willing to bet Amanda didn't approve.

Then again, his bets weren't exactly a sure thing since his luck had dried up.

"Whatever you say. I'll ride over to the courthouse with you. I've got to apply for warrants for Gallagher's friends in Queens anyway."

Rising, Duke grabbed his jacket. "Sounds like a plan."

They'd have Gallagher behind bars and three more suspects pending a hearing by nightfall.

Duke would be receiving the call for his promotion in no time.

Logically, he knew he should be pleased. Too bad his granddad had been shooting those lightning bolts at his butt ever since he'd walked out on Amanda.

And since Duke had indulged in a few viewings of *Amanda Does Manhattan*, he'd essentially been target practice for the old man. Nothing was going right anymore.

Now, a promotion and the satisfaction of another star on his chest didn't seem half as appealing as another night with Amanda.

Tonight, he was going to do something about it, because damn it all, once this case was sewn up in court, his luck was about to change.

AMANDA PUSHED HER way out of the crowded courtroom, eager to lose herself in the busy hallways. She had never been so nervous in her life as when she'd sat in the witness stand in front of a city judge. Even her interrogation with Duke while half naked had been a walk in the park compared to Victor's attorney's intimation that she was connected to the mob.

At least with Duke, she'd had the benefit of her lust to keep her warm.

On the witness stand, she shivered from the blasts of cold detachment of the people around her, Victor's blatantly disrespectful stare and the impassive audience provided by the woman who'd judged the case.

Duke's presence in the room made her even more nervous. He'd looked sleekly professional in his surprisingly understated jacket and tie, but the breadth of his wide shoulders still communicated a power and presence she knew she'd always be hard-pressed to resist. She'd been relieved when he'd risen just before she'd finished giving her testimony.

Now, she could return to her loft and put the finishing touches on her fall collection before she sent the designs out to be sewn. She'd be free from Duke

Rawlins now that the last string connecting them had been severed.

Except that he lounged against the wall not ten feet ahead of her.

Amanda sucked in a breath, his sudden proximity catching her off guard. Why did those smoldering blue eyes seem to follow her every move, seem to know her too intimately? She hadn't had time to give herself a mental pep talk about the dangers of men like Duke.

Even worse, she hadn't had time to notch her garters up a little higher.

Her pulse leapt at the sight of him, a little fluttering jump in her veins that annoyed and distracted her. Apparently he hadn't gone too far when he'd left the courtroom. He'd merely wanted to ambush her in the hallway. Why did he insist on pursuing her now?

"Hi, Amanda." He pushed off the wall as she slowed to a stop in front of him. "I wasn't sure you'd show up today."

"I told you I would." Would the man always doubt her integrity?

"I know, but the way I've been pursuing you lately, I thought you might blow it off just to avoid me." He shrugged, his shoulders tugging his shirt and tie slightly upward.

Only then did she notice the tiepin clipped to his conservative striped tie—a small silver star.

The nearness of his body did sneaky things to her. Her senses heightened, making her keenly aware of his slightest move. The scent of the starch in his shirt, the sound of new shoe leather creaking as he shuffled his feet, the warmth emanating from him at all times.

Amanda lifted her chin, willing herself to ignore the charismatic pull of a man who would only hurt her sooner or later. Today he hadn't trusted her to put in an appearance, probably because of her father's rumored mob connections.

Who knew what he would be suspicious of tomorrow? She couldn't stop being her father's daughter no matter how much it might please Duke Rawlins.

Besides, no matter what the rest of the world thought, Amanda knew her father had never done anything illegal. He might be guilty of occasional selfishness and maybe a little vanity, but he wasn't any more flawed than any other decent human being. One day she'd help the rest of the world to see that.

"I'd better get going," she said finally, needing to free herself from the magnetism of the man in front of her before she started noticing the musky scent of his cologne, the tiny nick on his chin he must have gotten from shaving.

Too late.

"Not yet." He reached for her, his hand stopping just short of her arm. "Please. Could we talk for a minute?"

Amanda didn't know whether or not to be grateful he hadn't touched her. She had the feeling she would start steaming if their bodies connected at any point.

While her impulses urged her to let Duke melt her

with his touch, her brain reminded her she'd never known him that well, that she'd allowed herself to be swept away by him last time.

"I don't think so."

He didn't step back, didn't afford her the breathing room she needed. He filled her field of vision, blocked out the institutional walls around them.

"Give me another chance, Amanda." He gripped her arms, gently, holding her in place.

Her skin sizzled beneath the crisp cotton of her shirt. Her body remembered his touch, craved more of it.

She'd forgotten how bold he could be, how he didn't waste words or hide behind a lot of polite chit-chat. So different from the people who moved among the fashion elite. "Why?"

One word was all she could manage now that his hands short-circuited her brain.

"Because I want to get to know you better. I couldn't get you out of my head the last few weeks, and I think there's more between us than either of us ever imagined." Intense blue eyes burned right into hers, his words tossing a match into the combustible jumble of her feelings.

"I can't." Or so she'd been telling herself all week when he'd left messages on her machine, or stopped by the showroom to ask her out for ice cream.

Duke would grow to resent her father's oblivious friendships with well-known criminals. Would he grow to resent her connection to her father, too? "My life isn't about taking risks, the way yours is."

Resolute, she stepped back, away from the temptation of his touch.

He shook his head as if he didn't believe a word she'd said. "Come on, Amanda, admit it. You want to take a few risks."

"Maybe," she admitted. "But not risks as dangerous as you."

His smoky 2:00 a.m. voice rolled right through her. "Then what about the window?"

She blinked past the sensual fog, thinking she must have lost a thread in their conversation. "What?"

He edged closer, his proximity far more threatening to her than any fashion critic had ever been. "The window you designed at your father's showroom. It's been telling me all about the risks you want to take these last few weeks."

Fire fanned in her belly as she thought of the mannequin swathed in yellow silk, dancing to the street music while her skirt fanned around her legs in a provocative swirl.

The woman in the window was captivated by life, unintimidated by the man in the starry tie who watched her.

Lexi had warned her that a New York police detective didn't miss a thing.

Amanda had designed award-winning displays for years without her father ever once commenting on their artistry or discussing a possible interpretation for her various vignettes.

Yet Duke's shrewd eye had seen right through to her heart in that window.

"One more date, Amanda," Duke urged, his chest looming inches from her. "One more chance to see what we could be like together."

Amanda's pulse pounded the answer toward her lips, urging the words of agreement to her mouth. But this time, she would be in charge and she was calling the shots. She'd be the first to walk away this time, because no way would she let him leave her again.

She wanted this man, but on her terms.

He made her feel risky, and uninhibited, and—curse his gorgeous hide—he even made her stockings start to slip.

11

TENSION GRIPPED Duke so hard he couldn't muster the good cop charm to save his skin. Weeks ago, between Battery Park and the zoo, Amanda Matthews had become important to him. And no matter how much he tried to leave her alone, to run in the opposite direction, she continued to be important to him.

He would deal with the fallout of her father's criminal ties later. For now, he knew his granddaddy's thunderbolts wouldn't quit until he'd made things right with Amanda. Without her, his luck had run out, his bed was painfully empty and his finger twitched over the Play button every time he got within ten feet of his VCR.

"What do you say? Can I take you out for dinner? Coffee?"

She watched him, studied him as if he were a mannequin she didn't quite know how to dress.

Damn it, he was prepared to do things right this time, to be a romantic kind of guy and stay out of her bed until she was really ready. "When was the last time you saw the other side of the East River, Amanda? I know a great seafood place near my house in Brooklyn."

He watched her brown eyes dance about, not quite knowing where to look.

Then, as if by magic, or some welcome stroke of his former good luck, she started nodding.

"Okay."

"Okay?" As if of their own will, his hands gripped hers a little more roughly than he'd intended, nudging her forward a step. He released her again, recalling their whereabouts and unwilling to make her regret her decision.

But he noticed a smile play around her perfectly painted pink lips.

Hot damn, but he couldn't wait to lick off every bit of that cotton candy lipstick.

When she was ready to let him, of course.

"I'll give us another chance, Duke, but on one condition."

He could respect a woman who knew how to negotiate. Nothing wrong with that. "Name it."

"We take it slow this time."

"Of course." He said the words automatically, knowing only a total heel would suggest otherwise, but he was surprised at how much he genuinely meant them.

She pursed her perfect pink lips. Damn, this would be a hard bargain to keep.

She tapped her chin with her finger. "Because you did say the whole problem last time was that we proceeded too quickly?"

Convicted by his own words. Maybe his luck was going to return in stages.

He stuffed his hands in his pockets. "That was part of it."

Amanda folded her arms in a pose that would look very get-down-to-business if it wasn't for the way those arms cradled her too-enticing breasts. "And what was the other part?"

Duke scrambled to uphold his half of the conversation, refusing to tick her off after the weeks he'd spent looking for a way to win her back. "I thought you only went out with me because you were thrill-seeking. Some women get off on the whole cop thing."

Amanda's eyebrows couldn't have shot up any farther into her forehead. She stared at him a moment, wide eyed.

Then, just as quickly, those same graceful brown eyebrows crouched down over her eyes with a look that made him stand up straighter.

"You thought what?" Her tone of voice did an excellent job of conveying her mood—appalled, offended, definitely mad.

"Some women are like that, Amanda," he submitted in his defense. "I went out with a woman who was only interested in taking a walk on the wild side. When you said all that stuff over breakfast about how you like that I was a cop—it made me nervous."

She studied him, assessed him, weighed his words. Duke shuffled his feet, waiting for her verdict.

Suddenly, she smiled. A happy, resplendent smile that gave him a tremendous sense of pride for helping to place it there.

"I didn't mean to hurt your feelings," she announced, taking his words and boiling them down to a phrase that made him sound like a candidate for an Oprah show.

But right now, he wasn't about to argue with an agreeable Amanda.

He edged closer, mindful of their public surroundings, yet wishing he could refresh her memory on the elements of their relationship that required no thinking, no fixing.

But he would be a gentleman this time if it killed him. "So now that we've cleared that up, what do you say we blow this joint? I need to pick up my car at the police station, and then we can be on our way. Did you drive?"

"Subway. Remember? It's a weekday." She hitched the strap of her purse up on her shoulder. "How about if I meet you later? You can finish your work and I'll squeeze in another hour or two at the showroom today."

"I'm thinking I'd be insane to let you out of my sight after waiting this long for you to say yes to dinner. We'll be there in ten minutes, tops." He would wait to tell her he needed to stop off at his place to change afterward. No use giving her any more reason to flee.

As she nodded, he steered her past a throng of reporters waiting for the verdict outside another court-room. Angling his way toward the front door, he no-ticed how heads turned when she walked by.

He felt the good cop charm returning, the lightness of spirit that had been missing in the weeks she'd been avoiding him. The smile he flashed her came easily because it flat-out felt so good to have her back by his side.

She sighed, her steps falling into sync with his again as they pushed through the front doors and down the main steps. "Do you always get your way, Duke Rawlins?"

"In this relationship, not half as often as you get yours."

Those sexy pink lips curved in a wicked grin.

She looked both ways for traffic as they waited to cross the street. Cabs and buses flew by, and Duke barely noticed with his eyes glued to her.

He tucked her closer to his side—he was being a gentleman after all—and guided her across the street to his car.

Once again, he couldn't help but notice how she caused heads to turn and people—men and women alike—to stare. Not that she was exactly a beauty queen, but something about the way she held herself, the way she wore her clothes, lent her a movie-star quality. She looked famous, like someone you should know from the tabloids, but couldn't quite name.

Just as he spied the unmarked, city-issued vehicle

and wondered why Josh wasn't there waiting for him, his cell phone rang.

Duke answered it, unlocking the car door and holding it open for Amanda. "Rawlins."

"Hey man," Josh's voice shot across the wireless, "I got tied up in another case because Judge O'Hare isn't in today."

Duke nodded, knowing they would wait for O'Hare to approve their warrants because of his well-deserved reputation as a cop-friendly judge. The request for warrants was good, but not rock-solid like they might need to be for another judge. "Is he there tomorrow?"

"Supposed to be. I'll be another hour or two here."

"I'm off the clock, then. I'll drop the car off and see you in the morning." Duke folded the phone and put it back in his pocket, happier than he'd ever been about waiting to make an arrest.

Usually, he couldn't wait to do his job, to keep the streets safe. Just this once, he'd rather let the crooks eat, drink and be merry for one more night if it meant Duke could have a few more hours with Amanda.

Duke winked at her through the windshield as he crossed to the driver's side. He didn't know how things might work out between them, but he sure as hell wanted to give it a try.

Amanda buckled her seat belt and waited as Duke slid into the car beside her. She couldn't believe she'd just let him back into her life after the way he'd walked out of hers, but she tried to tell herself this time she knew what she was doing.

Besides, she was having infinitely more fun watching Duke wrangle his broad, sexy shoulders in and out of police cars than she would be having at home.

She'd forgotten how exciting it was just to be around him.

He radiated energy and vitality, a thirst for adventure in life. For a woman who usually hid from life outside the studio, Duke seemed dangerous and at the same time, thrilling.

Duke switched the ignition on, lighting up the car dashboard with gadgets and crime-busting wizardry.

Fascinated, Amanda tracked the progress of flashing lights and intermittent beeps on the car's computer screen.

She shifted in her seat on the other side of the car. Two and a half feet separated them, but it could have been two and a half inches given the way her body shivered in anticipation of what might happen between them.

Her bare thighs grazed one another above the hem of her gartered stockings, igniting a heated awareness of the man who sat so close to her.

What would he think of her sexy getup if he uncovered the black satin garters teasing her legs?

She hadn't worn them for him, not really. Oh, she'd indulged in plenty of sexual fantasies involving Duke Rawlins over the last month. But when she'd slid the stockings up her legs this morning, she'd only been hoping to give herself enough confidence to make it through Victor's hearing. Something about seductive undergarments had always made her feel self-assured.

Except for the one time she hadn't worn clothes over them.

Smiling, Amanda thought back to the first time she'd met Duke. They were already pulling into the police station when she asked him a question that had teased her mind several times since then.

"Do you mind if I ask if there is a significance to the star-themed clothes?"

Duke stared across the console at her for a moment before he brushed idle fingers over his silver tiepin. "They're lucky stars. Sort of an Old West lawman thing, I guess. Cops have always worn stars."

Amanda nodded her approval. "They suit you well."

Duke shrugged. "Never gave it much thought."

"Nevertheless, you have a distinctive fashion flair."

He jerked his thumb toward the station. "Don't tell the guys, Amanda. They'd never let me live it down."

"Your secret's safe with me." The words tumbled from her lips, implying more than she'd intended. Images of pillow talk with Duke enticed, teased.

His blue eyes lingered over hers.

His hand snaked over the console to cup her cheek. Lightly, he brushed his fingertips over her skin. "We'll just pick up the keys to my car and then we're out of here, okay?"

Not waiting for her consent, Duke slipped from the car and rounded the hood to open her door.

Amanda used that moment to steady her emotions, to straighten her skewed skirt. She would not run away from this relationship. Not now. Too many times in the past she had taken the safest route out of personal relationships, had dodged commitments and confrontations by retreating back to her loft.

Not this time.

She planned to explore whatever it was she shared with Duke, to take charge of her personal life as resolutely as she confronted her professional goals.

Chanting that mantra in her mind, Amanda allowed Duke to lead her into the police station. She couldn't help but notice the possessive way he anchored her to his side as they navigated through the maze of desks and people.

Everyone greeted them.

Amanda didn't know if that was because of Duke's personal popularity or because the NYPD was just a very friendly place, but she found herself introduced to a dozen different people before Duke invited her to have a seat in his desk chair.

As Duke disappeared into the depths of the police station, misgivings set in. Was she making a big mistake by agreeing to dinner?

Should she just get it over with and tell him she wanted *him* for dinner and they could skip the seafood?

In a vain attempt to distract herself from the sudden

butterflies winging about her belly, Amanda tried to register the colorful swirl of her surroundings at Duke's desk.

Mets baseball cards formed a colorful place mat under a clear plastic desk protector, a postcard of Cincinnati taped on the side of his computer and a screen saver of John Wayne smoking a cigar in soldier's garb filled the space.

She'd barely taken it all in when a tall, uniformed officer plunked down in the chair beside her.

A tall, female officer.

"Hi, Ms. Matthews, I'm Rhonda Patterson." The woman stuck out her hand and smiled. "We met briefly after Victor Gallagher's arrest."

"Call me Amanda." Amanda responded automatically. She shook the woman's hand while recalling R. Patterson as the woman who had looked so strong and confident in her uniform while Amanda had cringed in her lingerie and trench coat.

"I see you've already met Duke." She pointed to the photo of John Wayne on the computer screen.

Amanda wanted to thunk herself on the head for not seeing the connection sooner. "We were just starting to get acquainted."

"He's not quite as charming as our Duke, but it beats a lot of the other guys' screen savers." She gestured around the desks with a broad sweep of her hand.

Only then did Amanda notice the proliferation of

pictures of women and guns on other people's desk-tops. ''I'd have to agree.''

''I just wanted to let you know I loved the clothes you designed last fall. Are you going to come out with another collection this year?''

Amanda stilled, her nerves about being with Duke quieted just a little. ''You saw my clothes?''

Rhonda smiled. ''Not that I could afford any, but yeah, I saw them. I think all the days stuck in a uni-form created an addiction to those cable fashion net-works.''

Pride fired through Amanda. She looked over the policewoman a little more carefully, now realizing the woman wore a designer original jacket over her uni-form. Apparently the woman was on her way home for the night. ''I wondered if anyone was watching those segments. I had to pay for the exposure, but I'd hoped it was worth it.''

Rhonda picked up Duke's stress ball off his desk and tossed it back and forth between her hands. ''Well you won me over. Your father's clothes are nice, but yours have a lot more youthful appeal. How long before you come out with something I can af-ford?''

Amanda fought the urge to fling her arms around the woman. She liked her clothes! Amanda had no idea whether or not she'd been making an impact with anyone outside of the Garment District with her small line of designs, but obviously she'd reached someone. This woman, who had no reason to flatter her, not only knew what she'd designed, but actively sought more.

She wondered if she would be able to stop smiling any time soon. "If your budget is anything like mine, probably not for a few more years. I need to build a name with the high-fashion magazines and the haute couture buyers first, to give me enough cash flow to try a ready-to-wear line."

Masculine hands settled over her shoulders as she spoke. Her heart lodged in her throat as her body keyed into Duke's presence, making her wonder how she'd managed to edge him out of her thoughts for the last two minutes.

Rhonda rose. "Well, I'll be looking for it. Good luck, Amanda." Her eyes flickered over Duke and she saluted him with a gunshot from her thumb and forefinger in the shape of a pistol. "See ya, pilgrim," she drawled as she sauntered away.

Duke squeezed Amanda's shoulders. "You ready to go?"

She nodded, peering up at him. "You're a John Wayne fan?"

"My granddad swore the only way I'd fall asleep as a baby was in front of the television, watching Duke Wayne." He winked down at her. "I sort of think he was just looking for an excuse to watch his westerns after a long day of dealing with three kids."

Amanda smiled to picture Duke as a child, absorbing the ethics of the Old West from the silver screen.

A thought suddenly occurred to her. "Is Duke a nickname?"

"You don't miss a trick, do you, lady?" Duke folded his arms across his chest. "You'd make a great cop."

It seemed like high praise coming from him.

"That doesn't answer my question," she persisted, curious.

"My birth certificate says John," he admitted, "but I don't know of anyone who's ever called me that. You ready to go?"

"Yes." Amanda lied, more nervous than she cared to admit. The thought of being alone with Duke again scared her, thrilled her.

She needed to change the subject—fast.

"Rhonda was just asking me about my next collection," she told him, rambling. "She must know a lot about fashion to be familiar with my designs. And I'll bet that jacket she's wearing won't be available in ready-to-wear for another year at least."

Duke punched in a few commands on the computer, inciting John Wayne to take one final puff of his cigar before the screen faded to black. "The Garment District is Rhonda's beat. She makes it her business to know everything that happens there."

He snagged a ring of keys out of a desk drawer, unaware his words had just utterly deflated Amanda's hopes that she was making headway in her career.

"She sort of keeps an eye on some of the designers—" Duke's gaze darted to hers.

He didn't finish the sentence. He didn't need to.

"Like my father?" How many other designers were suspected criminals?

Duke shrugged. "Designers lead very public lives, and sometimes that causes problems. Tabloid reporters loiter around the showrooms, the jet-set crowd attracts drugs dealers hoping to make big bucks...lots of things."

Amanda nodded. Her good mood vanished, but her determination to confront her father about his unscrupulous friends had just kicked into overdrive.

She wouldn't lead a life under suspicion and she wasn't going to be accused of guilt by association.

Duke Rawlins might be a brash, flashy guy, but at least he lived a life full of honor. Amanda wanted that kind of respectability, and she knew exactly how to get it.

By this time tomorrow, she'd be having a serious heart-to-heart with her father. And sooner or later, he would run out of arias to sing and he would have to listen to her.

She wasn't going to live in anyone's shadow anymore.

And for tonight, she intended to step into the limelight with Duke Rawlins as an audience.

12

DUKE CONSIDERED HIMSELF a "people person." Part of what made him a good cop was his ability to read someone else, an emotional sensitivity that made him alert to others' thoughts and moods.

But he had no idea what Amanda was thinking tonight.

He knew she could be open and down-to-earth—he had seen those qualities in her the day they bought out the vendors on Canal Street. Now, however, her reserved side seemed to have taken charge. She reminded him of the trench coat-clenching beauty he'd met at Gallagher's apartment, the untouchable mob princess and socialite he ought to avoid.

But that didn't stop him from feeling like he'd won a big victory today by convincing her to agree to dinner.

Duke downshifted his pickup truck as traffic slowed on the Manhattan Bridge. Thousands of other people were leaving the city at the same time, seeking their homes in Brooklyn and beyond.

"Is it like this every day?" Amanda asked, breaking the silence she'd maintained since they'd left the precinct.

She looked elegant and out of place in his truck. Her slim black skirt and oversize white men's shirt were simple enough, but Amanda had a way of wearing clothes that made her stand out. A gold pin in the shape of a dragon held her blouse together instead of buttons. She'd wrapped and tucked the tails of the shirt in such a way that she had plenty to cover her, but Duke couldn't help but think the whole ensemble would fall to her feet if he vanquished that dragon.

Not that he had any intention of trying.

Yet.

"Yeah. For me, it's worth it. I like leaving the city behind every night."

Amanda peered out the window at the East River. "Are you a native New Yorker, Duke?"

The question gave him his first clue to her mindset in the last hour. He didn't make it a habit of talking about himself, but she had told him she wanted to take it slow when she agreed to see him again.

That meant that they needed to get to know one another better.

"I'm from the suburbs of Cincinnati." Knowing that probably wouldn't suffice, he offered up a little more. "My grandfather was a cop in Cincinnati and I wanted to follow in his footsteps. Of course, when I was young and stupid, I figured I'd be doing even better if I fought crime in the Big Apple, so I moved here."

"Do you regret it?"

"Hell, no. I love New York. It's like the whole

world squeezed into a few square miles." He stole a glance across the truck cab to find her watching him intently. "I just meant to say I came here for the wrong reasons. I wanted to impress my granddad by working here, but I didn't realize for a few years that fighting crime here is pretty much the same as anywhere else. The crimes are just as frightening, human nature is just as unstable."

"You grew to like New York, but you see now that you could have remained closer to home?"

"I grew to like it, but I hope I didn't insult my grandfather's career by implying I was doing something bigger and better." He rounded the block to his house. "The restaurant is two streets over, but do you mind if I make a quick stop at my place first to change?"

She cast him a skeptical look. "Do you live far from here?"

He pulled into his driveway and pointed up at the big brownstone, but left the truck running. "Right here. But I understand if you'd rather not come in. I can be back in two minutes."

"You live here?" She blinked up at the house.

Duke looked up at the neat brick building, wondering what his simple home looked like through her eyes. "I've got three on this block. I rent out two of them, but this one is mine. It's not finished inside, but it's—"

"May I see it?"

"Sure." He answered too quickly, not taking time

to think about the ramifications of Amanda Matthews strutting her sexy walk through his house. She'd paint his hallways and imagination with enough fantasies to torment him all year.

Lucky for him he was a gentleman, damn it. He could handle a taste of temptation.

Killing the ignition, Duke jumped out and walked around the truck to offer her his arm. He refused to notice the way her skirt hitched up her thigh, offering a tantalizing glimpse of the honest-to-goodness stockings she wore.

The first fantasy already appeared, fully formed in his mind. It involved the truck's bench seat and a very unimpeded view of those stockings. Not that he would ever act on it.

Good cops were very proficient at being gentlemen, right?

"You'll like it," he informed her, talking just to distract himself.

He led her up the steps to the front door, already brainstorming ideas about how to treat her to a romantic evening. He had a bottle of great wine, if she was interested. And he could even show her the stars, if only she would let him.

Crossing his fingers for some of his luck to help him out, Duke scrounged for whatever charm he could muster. "It's got a showroom all its own, too."

Her curiosity piqued, Amanda followed him.

She sniffed the fragrant potted flowers in an urn on the brick handrail and wondered if he had planted them himself. She found it hard to envision the detective in gardening gloves, but she had to admit the combination of bright blue, purple and yellow flowers looked like something Duke would dream up.

No red geraniums for this man.

"Come on in." He flashed her a grin that made her think of spending all day in bed as he held the door for her.

As she sidled by him into the house, Amanda remembered that first time he'd held a door for her, when she'd been wearing next to nothing beneath her coat.

She'd thought her reaction to him had been strong back then, but she'd never imagined her longing for him would grow to the proportions that weakened her knees now.

If she hadn't been so committed to taking her time tonight, Amanda would probably already be kissing him senseless right now.

"Let me grab a couple of drinks, and then I'll show you the surprise." He tossed his keys on a curio cabinet in the foyer. "Make yourself at home."

Amanda wandered into the living room, charmed by the warm polished wood gleaming on the floor, on the wainscoting, in the ceiling molding. The patterned rugs, and elegantly mismatched furniture all used bright color. The deep flame color of the walls above the wainscoting wasn't gaudy, merely rich and warm.

"Don't tell me you decorated this place." She'd be a little disheartened if a New York detective could turn out this kind of decorating scheme when she couldn't manage to give her loft anything more than a couple of photos on the walls.

Duke returned with two glasses of wine and handed one to her. "You think I couldn't do it?"

"I don't know what I think, but you can bet I'd beg you to come work for me as a style consultant if you could pull this off." She sipped her wine. Smooth and warm, it held just the right finish without being too sweet or too dry. She smiled to think that, for all of Victor's snooty manners with the sommeliers of New York's fashionable restaurants, he'd never found her a wine this good.

Duke Rawlins was turning out to be full of surprises tonight.

"Actually, after I did all the woodwork, I scanned through a few back issues of *Architectural Digest* and pretty much ordered the room straight out of a photograph." He nodded toward the staircase. "Don't be too impressed. The rest of the house is a mess, and it will probably take me the next ten years to bring it up to speed with this room."

Amanda was comforted to see he spoke the truth. The other rooms in the brownstone looked more like Amanda's loft—scattered and disorganized, crowded with the stuff of his hobbies. Instead of fabric bolts and mannequins, Duke's home overflowed with saws and sawhorses, paintbrushes and ladders.

After an abbreviated tour of the other floors, Duke

led her up a third flight of steps and then shoved open a heavy door to the roof.

Amanda had been on the roof of her building before, and although the sights were interesting, the atmosphere of heating and air-conditioning units still made it a drab place to visit.

Not here.

A teakwood arbor and Adirondack chairs nestled in one corner of the roof, surrounded by potted trees and bushes. At the other end, a grapevine archway spanned a picnic table, all but hiding it from sight.

But the best part of the rooftop was the view.

Manhattan loomed on the other side of the East River, illuminated by the perpetual glow of streetlights and office lights. Night had fallen while they'd been touring Duke's house, and by now the sun was long set.

Raindrops lingered on every surface, hinting they'd missed a spring shower.

"It's incredible." Amanda walked to the edge of the roof to stare out at the skyline. "The city looks so glamorous from here."

"Glitzy on the outside, but lots of substance on the inside." Duke joined her, resting his wineglass on the low brick wall that ringed the rooftop. "Sounds like a woman I know."

He stood close enough to touch, his silver tiepin winking at her in the moonlight. It would be so easy to reach out to him, to run her lips along that granite jaw of his and forget all about her plans to get to know him better.

But she was determined to take bigger risks tonight.

"How do you know I'm not all about glitz and glamour?" She sipped her wine, foolishly hoping to find fortification in the mellow drink. "I've worked my tail off to create an image based on those very concepts."

"That's Amanda Matthews the designer, not Amanda the woman."

The damp night air blew between them, lifting Duke's tie and causing Amanda's blouse to billow gently around her body.

"They're one and the same." Awareness kicked through her as he neared, heating her skin and tingling through her veins.

"No they're not." He lifted her wineglass out of her hand and set it to rest near his on the low brick wall. "I went on a date with the woman, but I'm pretty sure it's been the designer who has been giving me the cold shoulder for the past few weeks."

Duke didn't want to rush her.

She'd said they needed to get to know one another better and he planned to make sure they did just that. He wouldn't take advantage of the moonlight to kiss her, no matter how much she tempted him.

She looked out at the Manhattan skyline again, but he could tell by the quick, shallow rhythm of her breathing that she wasn't unaffected by his nearness.

The notion teased his senses, making him wonder how long he could keep his hands off her if they remained here.

"Maybe I rely on my professional self to be strong," she mused out loud. "The fashion world is fiercely competitive. I guess I've had to adapt a certain attitude to hold my own." She turned back to him, her brown eyes reflecting the city lights. "They would have eaten me alive long ago if I ever let them see the real me."

Duke nodded. "Please say the real you is the one who knows the whole Mets roster and likes llamas."

"That would be me." She laughed. "I've never actually been to a Mets game. I ended up forming an attachment to the team because my father steals the style section of the paper every day. I'm stuck with sports or the front page, and since I refuse to read about murders and robberies, I started searching for sports news that would interest me."

"So you just chose the Mets out of thin air?"

Her grin was sheepish. "Their uniform colors were more interesting than the Yankees' blue and white."

"You realize that would be like me saying I liked the Amanda Matthews collection because the designer is a knockout, right?"

"A little insulting?" As the wind tossed her hair around her shoulders, Amanda tucked a few strands behind one ear.

He edged closer, unable to keep his hands off her another minute. Brushing his fingers over her arms, he lured her forward to close the remaining distance between them. "Come to Shea Stadium with me next week and we'll make you a fan for real."

"Will there be a next week?" Her unblinking gaze fixed him.

"I want there to be." He knew that much for sure. He didn't know what the future would bring for her father, however, and the shadow of Clyde Matthews and his mob connections still loomed between them.

But he didn't want to think about Matthews or his criminal friends right now.

She nodded as if content with their silent agreement not to talk about it. "So do I."

He wanted to kiss her.

He wanted to haul her into his arms and run like hell for his bedroom, but he wouldn't.

In a strangled voice he barely recognized, he prompted, "Maybe we should go have some dinner?"

He needed to get out of here if he wanted to continue in the gentleman vein.

But instead of answering, she used her pink-painted fingernails to scrape down the front of his chest just then.

Sparks flew from her touch, painting a trail of fire toward his...

She stopped too soon, teasing him with her fumbling fingers a few inches above his waist. "Maybe we ought to wait a little while."

He propped an eye open that he hadn't realized he'd closed and discovered her unfastening his tiepin.

If this was her subtle payback for his walking away from her, it sure as hell was working.

He gulped for a breath of air and tried not to touch her. She needed, wanted, to be in control this time, and he could respect that.

He just didn't know if he'd survive it.

She sheathed the pin and deposited it in his pants pocket before walking her fingers up his chest again.

Tension locked up every last inch of him. Maybe even a couple of extra inches, judging by the way his erection strained against her. "Honey, I don't know how much torment I can take. I've been thinking about you for weeks."

Slowly, she unknotted his tie and slid the silk back and forth over the collar of his shirt. A wicked gleam lit her eyes more than the city lights. "You deserve the torment after the way you ran out on me."

He groaned at the thought of erotic anguish at Amanda Matthews's hands. Not exactly a prison sentence, but he wondered how he could stand it. "I think you're letting Amanda the tough-as-nails designer take over again, sweetheart. I'm voting for Amanda the woman to make a comeback."

She unfastened the top button of his shirt, then another. Ducking her head under his chin, she breathed a hot puff of air onto the flesh she'd exposed. "Thanks to you, I think Amanda the woman is finally coming into her own."

He promised himself he would let her have her way. If she would stay with him tonight, she could definitely do as she pleased with his body. But he needed one touch of her first.

He clamped his hands on her hips and sealed her lower body to his, needing the pressure of her thighs against his.

Immediately he knew the movement had been as much a mistake as a relief, because now he only wanted her more, sooner.

Now.

Amanda thought she'd melt all over him as he crushed her up against him. She wanted to lure him, tempt him, make it impossible for him to walk away from her again.

But Duke was definitely doing some tempting of his own.

He nibbled hot kisses down her neck, plucked at the single pin that held her blouse together.

"Amanda the woman definitely has my attention," he whispered in her ear, his voice gravelly with the same need that gripped her. "I watch that striptease of yours over and over in my mind as if I had that videotape hard-wired into my brain."

Her skin caught fire and tingled with chills at the same time. The damp night air swirled around her, but it barely had the chance to cool her before Duke's touch heated her through again.

"You've seen plenty of me," she managed, gasping as he tugged open her blouse to the breeze. "It's your turn to reveal a thing or two, Detective. And I want the narrated version. The show *and* the tell."

He bent his head to her breasts, gliding his lips across each curve and moistening the edges of the white lace cups with his tongue.

She halted him with a hand on each stubbled cheek before he could reach the nipple, preventing him from inflicting the pleasures that might make her forget what she wanted from him.

His eyes darkened to midnight blue, smoldering her as he met her gaze. "You are turning into a force to be reckoned with, woman."

The notion thrilled her to her toes. "Let's start with the shirt, please."

His jacket long ago dispensed with, Duke slid his arms from his shirt and tossed it.

Amanda ate him up with her eyes. It had been far too long since she'd seen him naked.

His tie still dangled from his neck, but before he could tear that off, too, Amanda used it to pull him to her for another kiss.

His mouth opened to hers instantly. He claimed her lips for his own and feasted, chasing all thoughts from her head and leaving her only with the knowledge that she wanted him.

Now.

Her time for games had just run out.

13

DUKE PULLED AWAY by a fraction of an inch, allowing a whisper of the night air to wend its way between them. "I'm going to make a last-ditch effort to be a gentleman, Amanda."

Stars winked overhead, tiny lights in the sky she'd hardly ever noticed among Manhattan's dense forest of skyscrapers. Here, in a more residential neighborhood of Brooklyn, Amanda saw the night with new eyes.

"Don't you dare." She hooked one ankle around the back of Duke's calf and anchored herself to him. The inside of her thigh pressed against the outside of his, allowing her to feel the play of hard muscle beneath his trousers. "You're going nowhere."

His low groan satisfied her more than a feature in *Women's Wear Daily*. He wanted her every bit as much as she wanted him.

"What about the lounger six feet behind you?" he murmured, sliding his fingers down her thigh. "I could take you there."

She unhooked her ankle from his leg and shuffled backward, pulling him with her, but never breaking body contact. "Well why didn't you say so?"

When the backs of her calves bumped into smooth wood, Amanda turned around so that Duke stood in front of the lounger. Gently, she pushed his shoulders down.

"Make yourself comfortable," she whispered, hoping she didn't lose her nerve to push her daring to the limit.

"Comfortable is not something I'm really capable of at the moment." Still, he stretched out on the lounger and held his arms out to her.

She shook her head and allowed her open blouse to slither down her arms into a heap of white cotton on the cement. Cool breeze wafted over her bare skin.

He let out a soft whistle, giving her courage in spite of her jitters. She'd spent half a lifetime hiding her body under a mountain of clothes. It felt glorious to shed her clothes now, to claim pride in her feminine form.

She might still possess the generous curves shunned by skinny models, but Duke Rawlins didn't seem to be complaining.

In fact, the way his blue eyes fastened themselves to her bra, she had every reason to suspect he liked what he saw.

Nevertheless, she wasn't about to give him the whole show at once. She'd learned a thing or two about stripping in her awkward attempt to make a seductive video. Now she knew it paid to turn away from the audience when unfastening a bra.

Pivoting, Amanda gave Duke her back while she

unclasped the front hook of her bra and let the straps slip down her arms.

Was it her imagination or could she hear Duke gnashing his teeth as her bra hit the floor?

She peeked over her bare shoulder, her hands cupping her breasts. Not that he could have seen them anyway.

Sure enough, his jaw clenched to granite.

"Amanda." He practically growled the word at her.

"Yes?" She teased him with a smile, a wriggle of her bottom.

"I might have to take you in on indecent exposure charges unless you flash me a little glimpse, honey."

Oh, this was *too* fun.

"That sounds like blackmail to me. Definitely abuse of authority." Careful to cover her breasts with one arm, she twisted just enough to pull down the zipper on the back of her skirt.

"I think you're the one abusing an authority. I'm in some serious pain—wow." He stopped talking when she shimmied her way out of her skirt to reveal her black panties and lace garters.

She allowed her hands to fall to her sides and turned to face him.

His gaze made her feel beautiful.

"What were you saying, Detective?" she prompted.

He shook his head. "I was just saying that even if

your outfit was illegal five minutes ago, it's not any more. At least not in my book.''

She sauntered over to him, walking straight into the fire of his gaze. She wanted to feel the singe, to do a little scorching of her own.

He met her at the end of the lounger, pulled her to her knees and ground their bodies together. They fell back into the damp vinyl cushions, sliding their way around the chair. Her elbow bumped the armrest. His knee flung over one edge.

None of it mattered.

Amanda cared only for the delicious press of him against her, the crush of hard muscle against willing flesh.

His hands rubbed over her, branding her with his touch, claiming every inch of her.

He tugged the front of one garter strap.

"These are hot." Toying the clasp, he flicked it open with his thumb. "And very wicked to keep you locked away from me."

His hand roamed the front of her bare thigh, then slid over her hip to examine the strap on her backside.

She arched against him. "So free me."

And he did.

His fingers stroked her breasts, splayed over her belly, skimmed the lace of her panties until she lifted herself toward him, mindlessly seeking his caress.

She caught glimpses of the stars and the skyline through her slitted eyelids, pinpoints of light in a world that consisted only of him. The cool air wrapped around them, powerless to infiltrate the heat they generated on the lounger, turning to steam in the damp chill of the night.

Duke knew he'd never get enough of her. His hands skated over every silken inch of her, and he only wanted more. He teased her breasts, drawing her into his mouth while he squeezed the insides of her thighs, until he couldn't take another minute.

When at last, he slid one finger inside her, she came undone with a shattering cry.

He gathered her to him, shielding her body with his, absorbing her quivers until she quieted.

Only then did he ease his way out of his pants, fishing a condom from his pocket as he did. In a fit of hopeless optimism he'd shoved two in there when he'd left her to pour their wine.

He didn't have a chance to use them, however.

Amanda stole that task, slowly wrapping her hand around him to unroll the latex.

Her hair flowed around her shoulders like a veil, hiding her face. He guessed she was studying him, however, a notion which made his blood surge all the more.

She was on a mission to take control tonight and Duke would have to be a fool to object. He held himself still while she straddled him, but he lost it when she started to edge her way down his shaft.

Her silken walls clutched him, made him forget his determination to let Amanda have her way.

He rose up to hold her in his arms, steering their

movements until they found a rhythm to please them both. They rocked the lounger, the rooftop, each other until they soared together, straight into the stars that had witnessed the whole thing.

Duke buried himself in her, replete. Whole.

He held her among the lounger's cushions long after, until the chill began to penetrate his brain. Until the ramifications of the mind-blowing sex began to sink in.

Duke had no idea how an uptown girl like Amanda could hide such a brazen firestarter under her designer outfits, and he didn't care.

She'd stripped his willpower and all his best intentions when she'd shimmied out of her tight skirt, leaving him panting in her wake and trying like hell to keep up with her.

And she thought *he* was bold?

Amanda gave new meaning to the word.

Of course, she didn't look very bold with her hands curled under her cheek in sleep beside him.

In the dull glow of light from the street lamps below them, she looked like what she was—a sweet, smart woman who had the misfortune of being born into a mob family.

But Duke wouldn't screw up with her this time. Now, he had a plan of action.

As he carried her through the brownstone and tucked her into his bed for the night, Duke knew if he kept her with him, he could keep her safe.

She'd realize that her father needed to be responsible for his own actions, but that it didn't have to reflect on her.

Duke would make sure of it.

AMANDA AWOKE EARLY, especially considering the acrobatics of the night before. She gave a contented stretch alongside Duke, warm despite her nakedness, wrapped in his arms and blankets.

She wanted to lay there a little longer, but she knew she couldn't remain in a horizontal position with this man for more than five minutes without wanting him. And frankly, she didn't have an ounce of energy left.

Slipping out of the covers, she pulled on a T-shirt from a neatly folded stack of laundry on his bedside table. As she navigated her way to his kitchen, she found herself hoping Duke possessed the same good taste in coffee that he'd exhibited in wine.

The miniature grinder perched next to the coffee machine seemed like a good sign.

Within five minutes, she had a pot of mocha java brewing and two mugs waiting on the counter between the grinder and the answering machine. She could wake Duke up with the scent of great coffee, then jump him once she let him have a rejuvenating sip or two.

A perfect plan.

While she waited for the coffee, Amanda padded through the kitchen archway to admire Duke's living room again. She ran idle fingers over the oak wainscoting, trailed curious hands over a bookshelf that looked handmade. For all of Duke's modesty about the furnishings and decorating, Amanda knew he'd created half of this gorgeous setting with his own saw and a lot of talent.

Her eyes skimmed the titles in his bookcase—criminology textbooks and woodworking manuals—then alighted on the small television/VCR combo tucked in the shelf. Betting she'd find an old John Wayne flick in progress, Amanda turned on the TV.

The tape began to whir in the machine automatically, just as another machine beeped in the kitchen. Thinking her coffee was ready, Amanda reached for the television's Power button then paused.

An awkward woman was in the process of unzipping a black satin dress on the screen.

Amanda froze, paralyzed with shock to see her long-ago destroyed videotape come back to life before her eyes. She watched, mute with hurt and betrayal as the flirt on the runway teased and taunted the viewer.

Through the thunderous pound of a heartbeat gone rogue, Amanda heard a man's voice behind her in the kitchen. Ready to confront Duke about his flagrantly inappropriate viewing material, Amanda paused the tape, the image freezing mockingly on the screen. But when she turned, she was surprised to see the kitchen was empty. The light on the answering machine blinked, however, as the voice of Josh Winger boomed through the room on full volume.

"I've got dirt on Clyde Matthews—" the voice

announced as she wavered between kitchen and living room.

Still reeling from her discovery in the living room, she couldn't make her feet move. Even if her feet *had* been cooperative, she would have had to be a saint to have walked away from that message. And despite ten years of Catholic school, Amanda didn't even come close.

Josh's voice continued, "...some IRS figures that don't look right, but you'll have to tell me what you think. Give me a call when you get in."

In some back corner of her mind, Amanda noticed the coffee had finished brewing. With numb hands, she reached for the pot and filled the two cups she'd left on the counter.

She'd scarcely had time to mentally process what it meant to see a copy of her video in Duke's VCR. And now this?

Duke and Josh had been investigating her father. Did that make her evidence? An informant?

Or just sickeningly naive?

Regardless, Duke had betrayed her trust with the video. Quite probably in his investigation as well.

Cold settled in the pit of her belly. Her first instincts told her to flee, but she was no longer listening to the woman who hid behind her designer outfits.

No matter what the tabloids said about her father, no matter how many pictures the paparazzi had snapped of him with an arm slung around various gangsters, Amanda believed in her father's innocence.

He might not have won father of the year by sending her off to boarding school after her mother died. Amanda had been equipped with nothing but a damn sewing kit, for crying out loud. But his heart had always been in the right place. He'd spent the summers making up lost time, painstakingly showing her over and over how to piece together the tiny skirts she'd wanted to make for her dolls.

Her father might be too much of a showman. He might be too immersed in his art to pay attention to politics or being politically correct. But he was a good man.

Unlike the dishonest, deceitful guy she'd spent the night with.

Again.

She marched over to the television and stabbed the Eject button off with one finger. Armed with a video and a cup of coffee, she negotiated the stairs, ready to face Duke.

A man who happened to be a lying, two-faced detective who wouldn't ever have the chance to walk out on her again.

Because after one final encounter to settle the score, Amanda planned to slam the door behind her on the way out of his life.

DUKE SMILED BEFORE he even opened his eyes. The scent of mocha java teased his nose, while the warmth of the sheets beside him reminded him who had gone to the trouble to cater coffee to his bedside.

He couldn't think of a better way to wake up.

Well, maybe one other way. But he could convince Amanda to try out that method with him another day.

"I need to speak with you."

Amanda's all-business voice shattered his fantasies, forcing his eyes open immediately. She was fully dressed, right down to the golden dragon pin decorating her blouse. Her hair was already folded and twisted into submission at the back of her head. She thumped his coffee down on his bedside table and took a healthy step backward.

"What's the matter?" He sat up, keeping a corner of the sheet around his hips in light of her mood. "You don't like mocha java?"

"First of all, let me apologize for making myself too at home here this morning. In the time it took me to make a pot of coffee I ended up both hearing and seeing things I shouldn't have, and I'm sorry." She'd retreated to her boarding school manners, the ones she'd used to keep him at a distance that first day at Gallagher's apartment.

Only now, she wasn't hiding behind a trench coat. Oh no. Amanda looked very ready to do battle.

And he had the uncanny feeling her first victim was going to be a certain naked detective.

She withdrew one hand from behind her back and slapped an unmarked videotape on the bed. "Hope you enjoyed the contraband, Detective, because I guarantee it'll be the last time you see *this* woman naked."

A thousand curse words exploded through his brain as he realized what an ass he'd been. He'd been sleeping away, dreaming of slow morning sex with Amanda, while she'd been making him coffee and getting the rudest awakening of her life.

Why couldn't he have told her about it last night? He'd thought about it when they'd toured the living room, but he had wanted to wait until after they'd had a chance to talk. Once Amanda set her sights on seduction, however, he'd forgotten every freaking good intention he'd ever had.

He was struggling to frame an apology that didn't sound totally insufficient when she spun on one high heel and stalked out his bedroom door.

"Amanda, wait." He snagged a fistful of clothes from the stack on his nightstand and fumbled his way into a pair of shorts.

He tore down the stairs, amazed she could have put so much distance between them already in the spike heels she liked to wear. She tugged the strap of her purse up on her shoulder and reached for the door.

Duke levered it shut with one arm, inserting himself between her and the exit. "I'm sorry."

Standing face-to-face with her, he could see the pulse jumping in her neck, feel the subtle tremble of a body on fire with hurt and anger. God, he hadn't meant to do that to her.

"Amanda, I copied that tape at the station automatically, before I even saw what was on it. It's a standard procedure."

"Is it standard procedure to bring home your copies for private viewings? You certainly didn't bother to tell me that when you were acting like Mr. Honorable giving me my original tape back." She reached around him to grip the doorknob.

He had no choice but to let her go. He wasn't about to add holding her against her will to his list of infractions this morning.

That didn't mean he couldn't follow her.

Not wasting a second, he tied the drawstring on his running shorts and plowed through the door behind her. "It was an unethical thing to do," he admitted, clawing his way into the T-shirt he'd grabbed from the laundry pile. He bumped into the urn full of purple flowers on the stoop on his way outside. "And I had every intention of locking that tape in a desk drawer until after Gallagher's sentencing and then tossing it or giving it back to you. But I swear, Amanda, I couldn't get any work done at the precinct knowing that tape was in my desk. I saw the damn thing in my mind all the time, even before I caved and hit Play."

"You should have told me about it," Amanda shot over her shoulder, clicking her way down the quiet Brooklyn street. "It was a damned rotten thing to do, but I could have gotten over it if it weren't for one other thing. You can only betray my trust so many times, Duke. Maybe your grandfather shared this little bit of wisdom with you—'fool me once, shame on you. Fool me twice, shame on me.'"

Following her down his street, Duke winced as he stepped on something sharp. Too bad he hadn't found time to grab his shoes. He limped after her, damn certain he wouldn't see her again if he didn't pursue her now. "There's more?"

She paused to peer up and down the street, no doubt searching for a taxicab. "Your answering machine is right by the coffee machine."

That didn't sound promising. But it's not like he had any other woman in his life who might have called. Before Amanda there'd been a long dry spell. "And?"

"And I was still too much in shock from seeing my video in your VCR to politely duck out of the kitchen while your partner left a message about the investigation of my father." She picked up her pace again, obviously ready to walk to Manhattan until she saw a cab. Her long, angry strides radiated tension, anger…hurt.

"We aren't investigating your father," he argued, attracting the attention of an elderly woman in an orange caftan sweeping her front step.

The woman paused to watch the glamorous movie star walk by with her barefoot fan limping along beside her.

Great. Just great.

Oblivious to the scene they created for the few early risers that dotted the street, Amanda strode onward, her handbag swinging from her clenched fist with a viciousness that would surely discourage any purse-snatchers with half a brain. "Then why would your partner call you to offer up dirt on my dad?"

Her voice didn't quiver. Rather it shook with anger, a barely disguised urge to throttle him. Ten years on the police force had taught Duke to discern the difference.

It hadn't, however, taught him caution.

As long as they were having a no-holds-barred debate for all of Brooklyn to hear, they might as well confront the issue of her father. He sure as hell had nothing more to lose here.

"Maybe because your dad isn't keeping his hands clean." Duke offered. He was only stating the obvious, wasn't he? "Maybe his habit of hanging out with known criminals is finally biting him in the ass— butt."

She halted in her tracks in front of the bakery for just long enough to stare him down. Her cool gaze bore no resemblance to the seductive looks she'd flashed him last night. "Since when is it against the law to have criminals for clients?"

Duke noticed the baker set aside his rolling pin to watch the commotion outside the window. Duke and Amanda weren't being loud, but he had the feeling they created quite a picture.

"It's not. But your father doesn't do a damn thing to discourage the public perception of himself as a friend to the mob. If anything, he plays right into the 'Don of the Garment District' reputation."

"That doesn't make him guilty of anything."

"Bad judgment, at the very least."

Amanda planted her fists on her hips, showing him no quarter. "Still not a crime."

By now the baker's wife had joined him to watch out the window. Duke stepped closer to Amanda, wishing he'd stuck to apologizing and left the issue of Clyde Matthews for another day.

"I'm sorry about the phone call. And I swear there is no formal investigation of your father. Josh and I have heard he's greasing hands for extra protection and good favor among his friends. Apparently it's reaching the point that he's losing money."

Amanda shook her head, not backing down. "No. I know for a fact the business is losing money, but that's the effect of a slow season. My father will make it back once the fall collection hits the runways in a few weeks."

"So clear the air, Amanda," he challenged, desperate to convince her before he lost what could well be his last chance to convince her. "Take a look at his books for yourself and see if the old man is as innocent as you think."

She tipped her chin. "It would be worth it just to prove you wrong."

"I'm not." He tried not to notice the older couple who'd come out on their front stoop to take in the argument. Even the paperboy paused on his bike to watch the glamour goddess put the Brooklyn cop in his place this morning. Duke wondered if they were taking bets on the outcome. Hell, even he would put his money on the goddess. "Has it occurred to you that your father's reputation could hurt your business? Or that his gangster friends might expect you to treat them with the same courtesy he has?"

She gripped her purse so hard Duke guessed she was fighting the urge to swing it at his head. "You think I'm the kind of person who would work with the mob?"

He took a split second too long to answer. A mistake he realized he would pay for. Her disillusioned face said it all. Even with her lips still swollen from their night together, her collarbone bearing the rasp from his unshaven face, he understood without being told. They'd moved too far apart to put things back together. He'd known this could happen. He hadn't known it would hurt so damn much.

A flash of yellow moved by them on the street.

Amanda stepped off the sidewalk with one perfect leg and brought the taxicab careening to a halt beside them.

Duke scrambled to salvage what he could, all the while knowing whoever had bet on the goddess would win big. "It's not that I think you'd want to, Amanda, but you might be put into a position where—"

She held up her hands to thwart his explanation, backing toward the cab. "I'll talk to my father for my own peace of mind, and to prove you wrong. But I won't keep secrets from him."

"Amanda—" He moved to open the cab door for

her, at least, but the unusually solicitous taxi driver beat him to it.

Damn. Why did it feel like all of Brooklyn was on her side? Duke watched Amanda smile her polite thanks to the little old gentleman playing chauffeur and wondered if he should have taken a more circumspect position on her father's link to the crime world.

As she turned to slide into the taxi, her gold dragon pin winked at him in the sun.

Damn it, but didn't the serpent remind Duke how foolish he'd been to think he could vanquish any dragons for Amanda.

14

AMANDA DRAGGED THE last male mannequin into her father's showroom window, hoping one more plastic body would be enough to create the first vignette in her last-ever series of window designs.

Her father would have to find someone else to take her place now. She had her own company to run and she couldn't afford to spend any more time in a display window.

But she planned to go out of the window dressing business with a bang.

To that end, she adjusted one of the toy guns in another of the male mannequin's hands. Her series would be part political commentary, part Matthews family satire.

And part homage to Duke.

She'd be lying to herself if she didn't admit that she'd hated walking away from him. But what else could she have done?

He didn't trust her, didn't see her as one of the "good guys." She could paint herself with twinkle stars and he still wouldn't see her in the same light as his noble fellow police detectives.

In Duke's eyes, she was too tainted by the world

she'd grown up in. Perhaps by keeping a copy of her videotape, he'd continually reminded himself of the kind of woman he believed her to be—the sort who fraternized with criminals and did stripteases to entice them.

Still, a small part of her enjoyed the fact that he'd found her alluring enough to watch her video over and over. She had to thank Duke for giving her a new confidence in herself that she'd never had before.

Amanda hauled a box of silk ties into the window and started digging. She'd searched through two other boxes in an effort to find the right pattern to put on the mannequins representing the good guys in her window, but her father had a limited supply of outrageous neckwear.

The bad guys were getting black turtlenecks and pinstriped suits. Their enemies wore white cowboy hats with their dinner jackets, symbolism that would be blatantly obvious to even the hastiest passersby.

Too bad men in real life weren't so readily identifiable. Amanda had only seen the flashy exterior when she'd looked at Duke—an exterior that both appealed to her sense of style and shook it up at the same time.

But she'd failed to see beyond that to the high moral standards, the sense of nobility that was as much a part of him as the granite jaw and Sinatra blue eyes.

Too bad she'd fallen in love with that part of him along with all the rest.

Sighing, Amanda jammed a pair of sunglasses on each of the two good guys' plastic faces. They were the predators of the scene, the flashy avengers of the Garment District on their way to take down four perfectly pinstriped crooks.

She didn't want to upset her dad with the new window, just open his eyes to how the rest of the world saw him.

The movement of the curtain behind the window caught her eye.

"*Bonjour,* Amanda," her father called, angling his shoulders between the curtains. "How is your latest creation coming?" He peered around the display area with interest.

Amanda hadn't prepared herself to confront him today. But then, maybe if she kept waiting until she was prepared, she'd never really do it.

She took a page from Duke Rawlins's book and jumped in with both feet instead. "Good, Daddy. But this is going to have to be my last series. I'm getting swamped with fine-tuning my own collection for the fall preview next week."

She braced herself for an aria at full volume, but instead her father smiled agreeably.

"Of course, sweetheart. The windows can wait a few weeks."

Amanda gave in to the urge to grind her teeth for only a moment. "No, Daddy, I'm going to have to quit working on them for good. I just can't handle the workload of designing my own clothes and creating your windows, too.''

He tried distracting her without answering. First he offered her a cup of coffee. Then he tried calling in his bookkeeper, Karen, to look at Amanda's window. He even went so far as to hop into the window himself to make adjustments to the mannequins in the new vignette.

But Amanda ruthlessly steered their conversation back on course. ''You know plenty of artists who would love to work on your windows,'' she argued.

Her father pinned one of the mannequin's jackets for a better fit. ''None as good as you,'' he replied, his petulant frown not enough to detract from the hard-won compliment.

Amanda gave her father a hug, reminded that her father had a hard time reaching out to people. He had always preferred the world come running to him. ''Thank you.''

''Although, despite your artistry, I have no idea what this window is supposed to be saying.'' He pinned the other side of the jacket, blithely helping her create a window that would no doubt cause a lot of uproar in his life.

For the first time she realized how much faith her father placed in her, how much trust. So often she'd interpreted his silence about her projects to be an insult. But he'd only been allowing her room to create, trusting she'd find her own path instead of superimposing his artistic vision on her work.

Why hadn't she ever noticed that before?

"The display shows off a couple of menswear looks for the fall and also tells the world that the Matthews design house doesn't kowtow to criminals."

Her father's busy hands stalled for only a moment before he launched into a song from *La Bohème*.

Amanda tossed all the ties back in the box and stepped between him and the mannequin he worked on. "Daddy, I don't want our name to be associated with criminals anymore." She forged ahead, talking right on top of her father's Italian lyrics. "We are attracting too much negative publicity every time one of those mob henchmen shows up at our door and I don't like it."

He took his song down a notch in volume, a sign he might be listening.

"That means no more photo opportunities for the press the next time you see Freddie the Fish or Big Vinny or anybody else."

The aria trailed off to die a quiet death. Her father frowned, seemingly paying attention to her for the first time all day. "This is important to you?"

"Some people judge a man by his clothes, but others judge him by the company he keeps." She wondered if Duke's granddaddy was sending her telepathic pithy wisdom for the occasion. "I want to start gaining the respect of the latter."

Her father pinched her cheek in an ancient gesture that made her feel twelve years old.

"You sound just like your mother today."

His comment, however, made her feel strong and capable.

If only it weren't for the ache in her heart with Duke Rawlins's name written all over it, she'd call this day a big success.

Thinking of Duke reminded her of the one other piece of information she had yet to discuss with her father. "Daddy, do you think I could take a look at your books this week?"

"I'm losing money," he sang the words to the heartbreaking tune of the *La Bohème* song, distracted once again with adjusting the mannequins' clothing. "I'm going broke."

"Maybe I can help find the glitches," she offered, not wanting to delve any deeper into the story. Why bother her father with the suspicions of an over-eager police department?

Her father gripped her hand in his and poured out his heart in a rich baritone. "I wish you would. I wish you could. I'm bad with numbers, but you're so good!"

Laughing, Amanda returned to the box of ties, amazed how easily she'd accomplished all her goals with her father.

Had it been this simple all along and she just hadn't realized it? Or had she grown so much in the past few months that she'd finally learned how to coerce her father into conversation despite his determined efforts to avoid it?

Either way, he'd given her his blessing to review his books. Now, she would have the ammunition to prove her father's innocence and prove Duke wrong.

And sever the last tie between her and the flashy detective forever.

Funny, no matter how much she told herself she was better off without a man who would never fully trust her, the notion offered little comfort.

DUKE FLIPPED THROUGH the pages of Clyde Matthews's tax returns from the comfort of his rooftop deck, searching for holes and coming up empty-handed. He'd turned off the radio broadcast of the Mets game nearly an hour ago, but the silence did little to increase his concentration.

Who could focus with the memory of Amanda's rooftop show so close at hand? He couldn't look at the lounger without experiencing a fierce attack of longing.

But even worse than the sensual thoughts was the memory of her frosty goodbye.

He tossed the tax returns aside, frustrated on more damn levels than he could count.

He propped his boots on the low brick wall surrounding the rooftop and stared out at the Manhattan skyline in the bright afternoon light, searching for answers that couldn't be found in old W-2 forms.

His promotion had come through this week, along with Victor Gallagher's sentencing to five years on a handful of criminal charges.

Duke was now officially an NYPD Detective, First Grade. Yet the acknowledgement that had meant everything to him this spring now failed to make a dent in his dark mood.

Maybe because he was pretty sure his granddaddy wouldn't be proud of him right now.

In the course of the week, Duke had managed to alienate a woman who'd become frighteningly important to him. He'd wanted to spend all weekend with her after their night together, to stay locked in each other's arms until they had a better handle on just what was happening between them.

News of her father's potential crimes had put a quick end to that fantasy. But did it have to put an end to their relationship, too?

He'd tried to call her this week, but she'd gone back into evasive mode, hiding out from her answering machine and not returning his calls. He didn't know what he'd say to her, exactly, but he wasn't going to let her slip away without a fight.

Whatever he and Amanda shared, it didn't bear any resemblance to any other relationship he'd had in the past ten years. Maybe he'd fallen into the common cop syndrome of allowing his job to be his life. He'd always known his job would place a serious strain on any relationship, but it seemed inevitable that it would cause an all-out rift between him and a mobster's daughter.

The cordless phone at his side pealed through his

musings, a welcome distraction from thoughts that circled around and around Amanda Matthews.

But thinking about her all week didn't prepare Duke for hearing her voice on the other end of the phone.

"I've got your bad guy."

He stiffened. "Your father confessed?"

A long silence greeted his question.

"Amanda?"

"No, Duke. Despite what you believe, my father's not a criminal."

He gripped the phone tighter, finding that difficult to believe. Still, he didn't blame Amanda for not wanting to believe the worst of her own father. He just didn't think he could trust her judgment in crime solving.

"Then who is the bad guy, according to you?"

"It's a bad girl, actually."

Something about her sexy voice saying that particular combination of words brought to mind tantalizing images of Amanda in black leather. But he couldn't afford those thoughts. Not now.

"Who?"

"Do you remember the woman who came into the showroom with my father that day you talked to me about Victor's trial?"

Duke had a vague impression of her father's shadow scurrying around to wipe up coffee spills. "The bookkeeper?"

"Yes. Karen Wells. She's made a mess of my father's books and it looks to me as if she's been skimming cash ever since she started working for him.''

He found it hard to believe the little twit with the paper towels was tied to the mob while the bigwig designer who crafted clothes for every crook in the city was innocent. ''I hate to be the wet blanket, Amanda, but has it occurred to you she might just be fixing the books at your father's request?''

Amanda sighed on the other end of the phone. Duke remembered other sighs, the breathy variety that didn't sound so impatient.

It scared him to realize how much he wanted them back. If he listened to her cockamamie story about the mobster bookkeeper, would his feelings for her be clouding his judgment?

''Why would my father steal from his own business?'' she asked finally.

He paced the rooftop, hoping to clear his head. ''To cover up his payouts to the mob. They do business by demanding kickbacks, so it's possible that—''

''There are several entries for large sums labeled 'security,''' she admitted. He could hear her flipping pages of paper through the telephone. ''And my father doesn't have any sort of security system in place.''

Who needed security when they had the New York crime syndicate in their back pocket? ''Maybe you shouldn't be helping me with this, Amanda.'' What if he'd put her in danger by having her look at Matthews's books?

He plunked down into the lounger where they'd spent half of Friday night, wanting to think about her instead of the case if only for a few minutes. "I mean, I don't want you to hate me for uncovering the truth about your father."

"My father isn't paying off criminals." The bite in her words chilled him right through. "And I'm only too happy to uncover the truth. Do you think you could at least check out this Karen Wells person?"

"Sure." For all the good it would do. Karen Wells might be committing a crime, but it wouldn't come with half as much jail time as the man directing her activities would receive. But Duke couldn't begin to wade though the ramifications of that knowledge. Right now, he only cared about one thing. "When can I see you?"

Amanda pushed the Matthews's business ledger across her coffee table, clutching the phone in a death grip. She'd been bracing herself to ward off more insinuations about her father's guilt, so she hadn't been prepared for Duke's provocative question.

"I don't think that's such a good idea." Major understatement. The thought of seeing Duke put her heart in her throat.

"You're running away?" His words growled their way through the receiver.

"No, I'm taking a stand in several areas of my life, actually." Her eyes wandered around her loft, taking in the rolling racks full of samples of her fall collection. "You're one of them."

"You're taking a stand with me?" He sounded so offended, she couldn't help but smile.

Sort of.

It was hard to smile when her heart hurt with the knowledge that she would never walk her fingers over those muscular shoulders again, never thrill to the hungry way he stared at her less than perfect body.

"I don't think I'm going to get past the fact that you think my dad's a crook." The words didn't emerge in the light tone she'd striven for. Still, she forged ahead, thinking he deserved an explanation. "Besides, I have the feeling you aren't looking for the kind of relationship I am."

"Don't you think you're just looking for excuses?" A frustrated sigh came through the phone. "We are *not* having this conversation on the telephone."

Tears threatened to spill down her cheeks. Something she couldn't allow to happen unless she wanted to arrive at her first show of the season with raccoon eyes.

Still, she was unwilling to have this conversation anywhere *but* the telephone. Seeing him had a way of making her forget everything else. "I've got to go. I need to be at the Jacob Javits Center in less than an hour to start prepping for tonight's show."

"A show I noticed I'm not invited to?" She heard the disappointment in his words.

She swallowed. Twice. It had to be this way, no matter how much it hurt her to set him free. "I just wanted to let you know about the bookkeeper. It's up to you what you want to do with the information, but I'm going to make sure my father fires her.''

She could practically hear his teeth grind in the phone.

Good.

It made it hurt just a little less to know she wasn't the only one who was having a hard time walking away.

"Bye, Duke."

AMANDA'S WORDS ECHOED in Duke's brain as he sifted through computer files at the precinct two hours later.

He couldn't say goodbye.

Not then.

Not now.

First he would check out her bookkeeper, because Amanda deserved that much from him.

Then, he would figure out what to do to get her back. He wasn't the kind of guy who could wait around for the appropriate time to take action. Amanda might be all about subtlety and timing, but Duke had lived too many years on hunches and aggressive instincts.

He had to go after her. Had to see if they could outrun her father's influence.

But first, he needed to find out who the hell Karen Wells might be.

Her name and photograph scrolled across his

search screen in moments, an easy catch with her C.P.A. certification to help him track her down.

Duke scanned through other information—address, education, family ties, a photo from a news clipping in an accounting trade publication.

She looked sort of familiar with her dark hair and her bright smile.

When he reached an older story using her maiden name, his finger stalled over the mouse. Maiden name—Karen Patterson Wells.

He scrolled back up to family ties and spied her three sisters—Wendy, Jean and Rhonda.

Rhonda Patterson.

Duke looked over at the computer terminal across the corridor from his. Rhonda Patterson's empty terminal.

Was it possible Rhonda was the bookkeeper's sister?

Odd she'd never mentioned her sister worked for Clyde Matthews, given Rhonda's dedication to studying the designer's work in an endless search for possible evidence to link him to the mob.

A knot twisted in Duke's stomach as instincts kicked in. Hadn't Amanda said something about Rhonda's jacket being a designer original? It hadn't occurred to him before, but now Duke wondered if that was something the average beat cop could afford on an NYPD salary.

Adrenaline pumped through him, the familiar surge

of energy that came along with a big lead. Only now, the thrill of the chase was conspicuously absent.

In its place, he felt a crushing fear for Amanda. He looked back at Rhonda's empty terminal with a sense of foreboding.

He shouted across the precinct to the desk sergeant on duty. "Denny, who've you got down for security over at Jacob Javits tonight?"

Amanda would be vulnerable at the convention center, an easy target for someone who wanted to do her harm for snooping.

The aging sergeant moved his finger down the page of the logbook in front of him. "Looks like Kowalski is over there." His finger scanned laterally over the paper.

"Along with Rhonda Patterson."

15

CLUB MUSIC POUNDED from a state-of-the-art speaker system, bouncing a driving bass sound from one end of the cavernous convention center to the other.

Amanda forced herself to take deep, calming breaths, stopping in the middle of the backstage hub-bub for a moment to watch Lexi do a last-minute inspection of Amanda's runway models. Two girls needed makeup retouches, another one had the wrong color panty hose and one had forgotten to throw away her gum.

After ordering a communal bearing of teeth to be sure no one had lipstick on their pearly whites, Lexi declared them all ready for the show.

Amanda wished she felt half so prepared.

Lexi clicked her way over to Amanda in pumpkin-colored leather pumps that matched her bright orange leash for Muffin. "How are you holding up, girl-friend? You look like a wreck."

Automatically, Amanda smoothed a hand down her aqua minidress with bright fuchsia flowers. An un-characteristic choice, the outfit might have been an inadvertent attempt to brighten her world in the absence of a certain flashy detective. "Is the dress too much?"

Lexi twirled Muffin's carrot-colored leash. "You're asking me?"

Grateful for the laugh, Amanda peered down the runway from behind the stage's curtains. Her girls were on next.

"Guess I'm just nervous."

"Your designs are too fabulous for you to be nervous, Amanda." Lexi gave her a quick hug, mistaking the reason for the knot in Amanda's stomach. "I'm going to stake out a seat in the front row and prepare the crowd to be impressed."

Amanda watched her go, a pang of emptiness shooting through her despite the throng of people backstage.

How had her world grown so lonely without Duke?

She could surround herself with all the fuchsia and aqua prints she wanted and her life would still be a lot less colorful without him around.

To a certain extent, tonight's show reflected the excitement of the times she'd spent with Duke. Yellow silk now lined wool jackets that she'd designed earlier in the year. She'd replaced round buttons on all the fall coats with toggles in the shape of stars.

She had wanted to invite him tonight, but being together would only make her wish for impossible things. That Duke trusted her enough to believe in her father's innocence. That he cared about her enough to at least check out her father's bogus bookkeeper.

That he saw beyond her notorious family name to the person she was inside.

The music booming through the sound system changed to the big band sound of a Sinatra classic, cueing Amanda's models to hit the runway. The song reminded her of another man with heart-stopping blue eyes, but she couldn't think about him now.

As her moment in the spotlight arrived, butterflies filled the emptiness in her belly, along with a surge of hope for her fledgling designs.

Amanda high-fived the first woman in line and sent the lanky six-foot model down the catwalk.

For the first time, she felt no envy for the rail-thin feminine figures all around her. If nothing else came out of her relationship with Duke, she had him to thank for a newfound confidence in her body.

She was checking over her clipboard to be certain the clothes went on the runway in the right order when someone sidled up beside her.

Amanda looked up to see Karen Wells at her elbow, an earnest expression on her face behind her huge glasses.

"Hi, Amanda." She flashed a smile so brief Amanda thought maybe she'd imagined it. "I know you are busy, but I needed to talk to you in private."

Anger and resentment warred as she came face-to-face with the woman who'd probably been ripping off her father all year. Amanda gestured to the clipboard and the parade of models marching past her. "We're onstage right now."

Karen leaned closer. "I'm sorry. But it's about your father and his books."

That caught her attention.

Amanda tucked the clipboard under one arm. She'd planned this show right down to the last second, so she didn't really anticipate any problems. She definitely wanted to hear what Karen had to say.

Stepping into the shadow of a marble pillar for what limited privacy the backstage area afforded, Amanda waited. "Yes?"

"I hear you've been reviewing the books?" the woman hedged.

How had she heard? Had Amanda's father told her?

"Yes. I've been concerned about the money Matthews Designs has been losing lately." Amanda saw no reason to deny it. Sooner or later an outside tax attorney would sort out the mess and Karen would have to answer for her portion of the mistakes.

Karen lowered her voice. "We're not losing it."

Something inside Amanda stilled. She was more than ready for a little honesty here. "Not because of my father's business sense at least."

The mousy bookkeeper had the gall to roll her eyes. "We're paying off your father's mobster friends, Amanda. He's been doing it for years."

Instead of confirming her worst fears, Karen's words only strengthened Amanda's conviction that her father had no idea what Karen was doing with his money.

It seemed the bookkeeping twit had made some

very big assumptions about the Matthews family—
the same assumptions Duke had made. "Did you con-
sult my father about this before you started doling out
all his profits?"

When a few of the models turned in their direction,
Karen drew Amanda deeper into the shadows.

The Sinatra tune shifted into Duke Ellington, telling Amanda the show was half over. "I need to get
ready for the finale. Why don't we sit down with my
father after the show and talk this out? I'm sure we
can come up with a way to resolve any misunder-
standings."

Personally, Amanda hoped that resolution involved
firing Karen.

"You must realize we can't just stop making pay-
ments." Karen gripped her arm with surprising fierce-
ness for a woman of her size. "This is the *mob* we
are dealing with, for chrissakes. Organized crime.
People who can end your career—even your life—
before breakfast tomorrow."

"I don't think—"

One hand still locked around Amanda's arm, Karen
flashed a roll of one-hundred-dollar bills under
Amanda's nose with her other hand. "Besides, your
father would prefer you don't bring up this topic."

That pissed her off.

Boarding school manners didn't apply to this situation. Karen Wells had just crossed a line.

Amanda yanked her way out of the bookkeeper's
grip, righteous indignation firing through her even as

she knew she needed to get back to the stage curtains to prepare for her final bow. "Who the hell do you think you are to tell *me* what to say to my father?"

She was about to turn on her heel, away from the insufferable twit, when two broad arms locked her in a vise.

Two broad arms clad in a police uniform.

Her momentary relief was shattered by confusion.

The feminine voice accompanying those incredibly strong, uniformed arms only added to Amanda's puzzlement.

"Nice job, Karen," the voice intoned over Amanda's shoulder. "I told you she wouldn't go for the money."

Fear gelled in Amanda's stomach as she craned her neck to see Officer Rhonda Patterson squeezing the breath from her lungs.

Duke's friend? It didn't seem possible. Duke was so noble, so upstanding. He would hate to find out that one of his own, one of the good guys, was corrupt.

Karen stuffed the money back in her sweater pocket and shrugged.

Amanda wanted to scream, felt the ridiculous urge to call out for the man who should have been by her side tonight. Rhonda's hand covered her mouth before she could act on the impulse.

In the hustle of backstage chaos and models running at high speed back and forth from the dressing room, no one seemed to notice Amanda's distress in the shadow of one marble pillar.

"If her father is clean in spite of all his gangster friends," Rhonda hissed at the bookkeeper, "doesn't it make sense that his sheltered daughter would be all the more ethical?"

A moment of satisfaction swirled through Amanda even as she feared for her safety. Rhonda's words confirmed her father's innocence.

"Now how are we supposed to shut her up?" Rhonda's words mingled with the show commentator's voice praising the new fall collection by Amanda Matthews over the sound system.

Thunderous applause drowned out all other sound, an erratic pulsing beat that hammered through the convention center and echoed the thump of her heart.

The M.C.'s voice overrode the applause. "Ladies and gentlemen, presenting Amanda Matthews!"

DUKE FIDGETED IN HIS seat next to Lexi, the announcer's voice ringing in his ears. Any second and he would see Amanda.

Amanda's best friend had convinced him not to go backstage when he'd charged through the fashion show audience a few minutes before. Lexi had given him Muffin's seat, a fact which hadn't pleased him or the dog.

Duke needed to see Amanda.

Now.

He'd filched a squad car so he could fly through

city traffic with the siren blaring. But when he'd arrived at the fashion exhibition, Lexi assured him Amanda was fine and that he should wait until she finished up her show.

He kept telling himself she was safe, but he wouldn't relax until he saw her.

When the announcer finally called her to the stage to take a bow, Duke realized he'd been holding his breath.

The gaunt models wearing Amanda Matthews's clothes lined either side of the runway and started clapping, clearing a space for the designer to take center stage.

Amanda deserved it.

She'd worked hard for this moment, and had succeeded despite her father's demands on her time and Duke's insistence that Clyde Matthews's activities warranted investigation.

Too bad Amanda hadn't appeared to take the bows she'd earned.

Dread—a foreboding ten times stronger than what he'd felt at the precinct—kicked in.

His instincts fired to life before the anorexic army quit clapping. Duke vaulted onto the stage as the announcer called for Amanda again, as the crowd of society's fashion elite gasped and squawked at him.

He shoved his way behind the curtains, his eyes struggling to adjust to the dim light.

From somewhere behind the throng of people, Duke heard a muffled cry.

Dodging the stage security and an angry-looking man with a headset and clipboard, Duke followed the sound. He turned, shoved, ran around anyone in his way.

A flash of aqua and killer thigh caught his eye through the archway of a door already starting to close.

He knew those legs.

Duke sprinted to the door as it closed, reaching the exit in time to hear a feminine voice howl in pain.

"You bitch!" The voice didn't belong to Amanda, but sounded familiar all the same.

He plowed into a back room cluttered with makeup mirrors and folding chairs. Among the sprawl of rolling racks and abandoned hangers in the makeshift dressing room, Duke nearly slammed into Officer Rhonda Patterson hopping around on one foot.

"I think she broke my toe," Rhonda announced, her face broadcasting a bright red imprint of an angry palm as she glared across the room.

Duke turned to see the object of Rhonda's evil eye, only to find a curvaceous knockout in fuchsia high heels.

"Amanda." He said her name and his whole damn world fell into place. He never would have expected this gorgeous creature to be a bulldog in disguise.

But Amanda smiled back at him with her teenage fantasy grin and nary a hair out of place while one of New York's finest limped around the dressing room, cursing up a blue streak.

For the first time in his whole life, he didn't know what to say. Something about Amanda made his blood run hot, his mouth go dry, and his heart stick in his damn throat.

Good cop charm wasn't even an option.

Amanda smoothed her dress and patted her styled hair, her hands suddenly a flurry of motion. "She started it," she stated flatly, nodding toward Rhonda.

Relief flooded through him, soothing the nerves that had been wired from the moment he'd found out Amanda's thieving bookkeeper was tied to a New York cop.

"I know who started it." He didn't have any intention of letting Rhonda or her sister escape tonight. Duke had already called Josh during the drive over, and his partner would be here any minute to help deal with the mess. "You let me worry about sorting out what happened."

He suppressed the urge to hug her, to kiss her, to tell her how much he'd realized he loved her. Right now, she needed to hear something even more important.

Taking her shoulders, he guided her back toward the runway. Without saying a word, he marched her steadily forward, not daring to give into the desire to trail his hands all over her smooth skin and soak in the feel of her softness.

They passed some of Amanda's models behind the curtains, models who quickly turned their skinny hides to hightail back to their positions.

Duke didn't quit, didn't let Amanda pause, until they hit the catwalk.

"They want to meet the real you," he whispered in her ear, powerless to resist the compulsion to brush his lips over her warm skin for a fraction of a second.

Then he gave her a gentle shove, pushing her into the limelight to take all the credit she deserved.

AMANDA'S PHONE RANG off the hook the next day, but none of the calls delivered the voice she wanted to hear most.

All of New York wanted an Amanda Matthews original.

Half the city clamored for her clothes because her designs were being touted by every fashion magazine on the newsstands. The other half of the city wanted an Amanda Matthews outfit because of the notoriety she'd gained with the much-inflated tale of her triumph over an evil bookkeeper and a cop on the take.

She was the flavor of the minute in a city that would move on to something else by sundown.

But she was having a hard time enjoying her newfound cache while preoccupied with thoughts of Duke.

He'd walked into her nightmare in the nick of time, white stars blazing against the blue cotton of some sports team's T-shirt.

Duke Rawlins—all the magnetism of John Wayne in a new and improved package.

Her hero had arrived.

She'd wanted to plaster herself all over him then and there. But for one frozen moment she hadn't been sure if he would believe her story, if he'd trust a Matthews's word over the lady cop's.

Turned out he did.

The memory of his trust warmed her. Although he had already guessed Officer Patterson was up to no good by the time he'd arrived last night, Duke could have easily suspected Amanda or her family of having a hand in the criminal activity.

He hadn't.

Duke had simply made his arrests and ridden into the sunset, a flurry of drooling models in his wake. He'd insisted Amanda stay at the convention center and reap the rewards of her new fame. A gesture which had touched her even though it robbed them of the opportunity to talk.

But it didn't explain why he hadn't called her today.

The buzzer on the back entrance to her father's showroom went off, a momentary break in the monotony of the ringing telephone.

Hope leaped through her, the same ridiculous eagerness that had prodded her steps to the phone the first ten times it rang this morning. She refused to open the door and be disappointed, however, so she called her father away from his sketch pad in the corner of the showroom.

"Daddy, someone's at the door," she called, picking up the ringing phone so it wouldn't look like she was being too lazy—or too anxious—to answer the buzzer for herself.

Frowning, her father tossed his pencil aside. "I'm not talking to any reporters," he grumbled.

The newspapers had all been running stories on Clyde Matthews's "break" with the mob, a fact which had brought him a few disgruntled phone calls from crime bosses worried they wouldn't be able to buy their favorite suits anymore.

Amanda and her father had agreed the showroom could be open to anyone, but there wouldn't be any more photos with gangsters, and that the Matthews's design house would actively pursue more public-friendly clients.

Like police detectives, maybe, Amanda had secretly thought.

She could see Duke in a Clyde Matthews suit. With the appropriate celestial accoutrements, of course. Would he ever wear something her father designed? Or would he opt to keep his distance from Amanda's world?

She strained her ears to hear who was at the back door. The caller on the other end of the phone wanted to order the aqua dress Amanda had worn the previous night, along with the same dress in other prints.

Amanda took the woman's name and number, unwilling to lose important sales because all she could think about was Duke.

"Amanda," her father called from the back. "I've

got a customer who wants the white cowboy hat in the window. I don't even make a cowboy hat, do I?''

A tiny thrill zinged through her despite her best effort to suppress the hope, the excitement.

How many residents of the Big Apple would honestly walk into Clyde Matthews's upscale showroom requesting a cowboy hat?

She replaced the telephone receiver and hopped off the stool where she'd been sitting. A butterfly battalion fluttered through her belly.

"It's really more of a decoration," she started, stepping tentatively onto the showroom floor just as her father and his customer rounded the tie rack.

A very broad-shouldered customer with drop-dead blue eyes.

Duke.

"It's not for me," Duke protested, holding up his hands in the surrender position while her father relegated himself to the background. "But I'd like to give one to a friend of mine."

Amanda's pulse hammered into overtime, aggravated by the butterflies and the hope that Duke Rawlins might be in her life again for good this time. "A gift?"

Duke shrugged, accentuating the sinews beneath the perfectly tailored lines of his surprisingly conservative suit. His silver tiepin winked from the smooth silk banner of a yellow-striped tie. "Yeah. Sort of as a gag to let her know she's one of the good guys."

The lump in Amanda's throat prevented her from talking.

Acceptance radiated from Duke as he laid gentle hands on her shoulders. What surprised her was the worry lurking in his blue eyes.

A fear she wouldn't accept him in return?

"I'm sorry I didn't trust you, Amanda." The tone of his voice conveyed sincerity, the volume said he wanted this message to be overheard by any eccentric designers who happened to be humming in their vicinity.

"Maybe the Matthews's image—my image—needed a little polishing," she admitted.

"No." He clutched her shoulders just a little tighter, impressing his message with his touch. "I should have seen beyond the trappings to the woman underneath. I'll be the first to admit I didn't look beyond Rhonda's uniform to trust her, and I didn't look beyond your family reputation to *not* trust you." He shook his head. "Big mistake on both counts."

She liked the direction of this conversation.

Folding her arms over her chest, she nodded. "A very big mistake."

His hands slid down her shoulders, igniting a wave of pleasing shivers all over her body. His grin unfurled, bringing a healthy dose of signature Duke charm along with it. "Lucky for me, I've thought of a way to make up for it."

"Oh really?" Anticipation danced through her veins.

He reached into his pocket and pulled out a lovely length of creamy antique lace tied in a knot. "I'm going to ply you with gifts."

Confused, Amanda reached for his odd offering. "It's a pretty scarf," she started, not sure what else to say about a piece of lace tied in a knot.

"The best Canal Street had to offer this morning," he continued. If he noticed her awkward response, he didn't remark on it. "But that's just the wrapper for the other gift."

The butterflies in her stomach went into action again.

She squinted at the knot, trying to see what secrets it might contain. She didn't dare to look at him for fear her hopes would be written too plainly in her eyes. "Must be a pretty small gift considering it was such a big mistake."

Her hands trembled as she picked at the knot until Duke's big fingers took over the task.

She couldn't breathe as she slid the ends of the fabric apart and found a sturdy golden band woven with Celtic knots.

A ring.

Tears sprang to her eyes.

"It's another Canal Street special. I got it for you until you can help me shop for the real thing."

She blinked back the tears, wanting to be sure she understood before she lost her heart to this man forever. With what little bit of voice she could scavenge in the midst of a huge well of emotion, she asked, "What real thing?"

"A wedding ring." Duke curled his hand around hers, effectively closing her hand around the scarf and the ring. "That's my most important gift, honey." He pulled her against him, crushing her in an embrace that promised more than a lifetime of toe-curling sex. "What I really want to give you is me." He tipped her chin with one finger. "If you'll have me?"

The nervous butterflies turned into a joy so sweet, so hot, she wanted to melt right into him.

"Yes," she breathed the word against his mouth as he lowered his lips to hers for a kiss.

He sealed their bodies together, ran possessive hands over her back and around her waist.

Amanda threaded her fingers through his spiky hair, dragging him even closer.

The upbeat cadence of a happy tune whistled through her spinning consciousness.

A none-too-subtle sign of her father's approval.

Duke peeled himself away from her, probably following those frustrating gentlemanly instincts again.

Much to her satisfaction, however, his blue gaze sizzled in spite of his restrained hands.

While she was in the middle of returning every one of his hot, wait-until-I-get-you-alone looks, Amanda suddenly became aware of an oversize hat being stuffed unceremoniously onto her head.

Her father stepped in between her and Duke to tip

up the brim of the white cowboy hat Duke had been looking for.

"She looks good in white, no?" her father remarked, studying Amanda critically.

Subtlety had never been Clyde Matthews's strong suit.

Come to think of it, Duke and her father had something in common after all.

Duke cleared his throat. "If that's a hint, Mr. Matthews, don't worry. I was just in the middle of proposing."

Her father harrumphed. "What I just saw didn't look like a proposal. But if there's a wedding on the way—"

"There is," Duke and Amanda answered in perfect time.

"Excellent." Her father beamed. He plucked the hat from Amanda's head and plopped it on his own. "I can be one of the good guys again now that my daughter has a detective to watch over her." He winked at Amanda. "You have to admit having a father with connections has kept the riffraff away for the last few years."

Amanda groaned, but she thought she spied a hint of male understanding in Duke's eyes. "Daddy you promised—"

The designer nodded. "No more gangsters." He held out his arms to Amanda and hugged her. "And no more chaperones, because I'm on my way out. Congratulations, princess."

Embarrassment heated her cheeks, but she squeezed her father right back. "Thank you, Daddy."

After a quick shake of Duke's hand and an announcement that he was leaving for an early dinner, Clyde Matthews left them alone, singing "Love is a Many-Splendored Thing" as he ambled out onto the streets of New York.

Leaving them alone.

Anticipation made her every nerve tingle along with the small bell tied to the closing showroom door.

She watched Duke walk over to the entrance and pull the blinds with slow deliberation. The sound of the bolt sliding into the lock had the hair on her neck standing on end.

"I want you, Amanda." The smoky timbre of his voice told her he'd missed her as much as she'd missed him. "Too much to wait for the wedding, no matter what your father says."

Opening her fist, Amanda withdrew the gift she'd been holding.

"That's okay. I've got a ring that says you aren't going anywhere." She slid the gold band on one finger, then wriggled another in a distinct invitation to come closer.

Duke moved nearer until their bodies brushed, teased against one another. "I'm all yours."

"All mine?" Deliberately, she walked her fingers down the length of his tie, pausing near his belt.

"Completely." He reached for her, but she manacled his wrists with her hands.

"Good. Because I've got some ideas for a new video I'd like to make." She danced backward, toward the stairs to her loft.

He followed her, his long stride closing the space between them as fast as her narrow skirt would allow her to escape.

"I'd love to hear all about your ideas, Amanda."

And she was going to love teasing this man for the rest of her life.

"Really?" She cast a heated look over her shoulder. "I keep thinking about an interrogation scene between a bold detective and a half-naked woman. Or maybe a strip search...."

His low growl drowned out anything else she might have suggested. He caught her before she hit the stairs and threatened her with a sensual reenactment of her every wish.

Amanda couldn't wait to let the games begin.

The Cities
New York, Houston, Seattle

The Singles
Dating dropouts
Chelsea Brockway, Gwen Kempner, Kate Talavera

The Solution—THE SKIRT!

Can a skirt really act as a man magnet? These three
hopeful heroines are dying to find out! But once
they do, how will they know if the men of their
dreams really want *them*...or if the guys are just
making love under the influence?

Find out in...

Temptation #860—*MOONSTRUCK IN MANHATTAN*
by Cara Summers, December 2001

Temptation #864—*TEMPTED IN TEXAS*
by Heather MacAllister, January 2002

Temptation #868—*SEDUCED IN SEATTLE*
by Kristin Gabriel, February 2002

 ***It's a dating
wasteland out there!***

This Mother's Day Give Your Mom 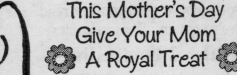 A Royal Treat

Win a fabulous one-week vacation in Puerto Rico for you and your mother at the luxurious Inter-Continental San Juan Resort & Casino. The prize includes round trip airfare for two, breakfast daily and a mother and daughter day of beauty at the beachfront hotel's spa.

INTER·CONTINENTAL
San Juan
RESORT & CASINO

Here's all you have to do:

Tell us in 100 words or less how your mother helped with the romance in your life. It may be a story about your engagement, wedding or those boyfriends when you were a teenager or any other romantic advice from your mother. The entry will be judged based on its originality, emotionally compelling nature and sincerity. See official rules on following page.

Send your entry to:

Mother's Day Contest

In Canada	**In U.S.A.**
P.O. Box 637	P.O. Box 9076
Fort Erie, Ontario	3010 Walden Ave.
L2A 5X3	Buffalo, NY
	14269-9076

Or enter online at www.eHarlequin.com

PRROY

HARLEQUIN MOTHER'S DAY CONTEST 2216
OFFICIAL RULES
NO PURCHASE NECESSARY TO ENTER

Two ways to enter:

• **Via The Internet:** Log on to the Harlequin romance website (www.eHarlequin.com) anytime beginning 12:01 a.m. E.S.T., January 1, 2002 through 11:59 p.m. E.S.T., April 1, 2002 and follow the directions displayed on-line to enter your name, address (including zip code), e-mail address and in 100 words or fewer, describe how your mother helped with the romance in your life.

• **Via Mail:** Handprint (or type) on an 8 1/2" x 11" plain piece of paper, your name, address (including zip code) and e-mail address (if you have one), and in 100 words or fewer, describe how your mother helped with the romance in your life. Mail your entry via first-class mail to: Harlequin Mother's Day Contest 2216, (in the U.S.) P.O. Box 9076, Buffalo, NY 14269-9076; (in Canada) P.O. Box 637, Fort Erie, Ontario, Canada L2A 5X3.

For eligibility, entries must be submitted either through a completed Internet transmission or postmarked no later than 11:59 p.m. E.S.T., April 1, 2002 (mail-in entries must be received by April 9, 2002). Limit one entry per person, household address and e-mail address. On-line and/or mailed entries received from persons residing in geographic areas in which entry is not permissible will be disqualified.

Entries will be judged by a panel of judges, consisting of members of the Harlequin editorial, marketing and public relations staff using the following criteria:
- Originality - 50%
- Emotional Appeal - 25%
- Sincerity - 25%

In the event of a tie, duplicate prizes will be awarded. Decisions of the judges are final.

Prize: A 6-night/7-day stay for two at the Inter-Continental San Juan Resort & Casino, including round-trip coach air transportation from gateway airport nearest winner's home (approximate retail value: $4,000). Prize includes breakfast daily and a mother and daughter day of beauty at the beachfront hotel's spa. Prize consists of only those items listed as part of the prize. Prize is valued in U.S. currency.

All entries become the property of Torstar Corp. and will not be returned. No responsibility is assumed for lost, late, illegible, incomplete, inaccurate, non-delivered or misdirected mail or misdirected e-mail, for technical, hardware or software failures of any kind, lost or unavailable network connections, or failed, incomplete, garbled or delayed computer transmission or any human error which may occur in the receipt or processing of the entries in this Contest.

Contest open only to residents of the U.S. (except Colorado) and Canada, who are 18 years of age or older and is void wherever prohibited by law; all applicable laws and regulations apply. Any litigation within the Province of Quebec respecting the conduct or organization of a publicity contest may be submitted to the Régie des alcools, des courses et des jeux for a ruling. Any litigation respecting the awarding of a prize may be submitted to the Régie des alcools, des courses et des jeux only for the purpose of helping the parties reach a settlement. Employees and immediate family members of Torstar Corp. and D.L. Blair, Inc., their affiliates, subsidiaries and all other agencies, entities and persons connected with the use, marketing or conduct of this Contest are not eligible to enter. Taxes on prize are the sole responsibility of winner. Acceptance of any prize offered constitutes permission to use winner's name, photograph or other likeness for the purposes of advertising, trade and promotion on behalf of Torstar Corp., its affiliates and subsidiaries without further compensation to the winner, unless prohibited by law.

Winner will be determined no later than April 15, 2002 and be notified by mail. Winner will be required to sign and return an Affidavit of Eligibility form within 15 days after winner notification. Non-compliance within that time period may result in disqualification and an alternate winner may be selected. Winner of trip must execute a Release of Liability prior to ticketing and must possess required travel documents (e.g. Passport, photo ID) where applicable. Travel must be completed within 12 months of selection and is subject to traveling companion completing and returning a Release of Liability prior to travel; and hotel and flight accommodations availability. Certain restrictions and blackout dates may apply. No substitution of prize permitted by winner. Torstar Corp. and D.L. Blair, Inc., their parents, affiliates, and subsidiaries are not responsible for errors in printing or electronic presentation of Contest, or entries. In the event of printing or other errors which may result in unintended prize values or duplication of prizes, all affected entries shall be null and void. If for any reason the Internet portion of the Contest is not capable of running as planned, including infection by computer virus, bugs, tampering, unauthorized intervention, fraud, technical failures, or any other causes beyond the control of Torstar Corp. which corrupt or affect the administration, secrecy, fairness, integrity or proper conduct of the Contest, Torstar Corp. reserves the right, at its sole discretion, to disqualify any individual who tampers with the entry process and to cancel, terminate, modify or suspend the Contest or the Internet portion thereof. In the event the Internet portion must be terminated a notice will be posted on the website and all entries received prior to termination will be judged in accordance with these rules. In the event of a dispute regarding an on-line entry, the entry will be deemed submitted by the authorized holder of the e-mail account submitted at the time of entry. Authorized account holder is defined as the natural person who is assigned to an e-mail address by an Internet access provider, on-line service provider or other organization that is responsible for arranging e-mail address for the domain associated with the submitted e-mail address. Torstar Corp. and/or D.L. Blair Inc. assumes no responsibility for any computer injury or damage related to or resulting from accessing and/or downloading any sweepstakes material. Rules are subject to any requirements/limitations imposed by the FCC. **Purchase or acceptance of a product offer does not improve your chances of winning.**

For winner's name (available after May 1, 2002), send a self-addressed, stamped envelope to: Harlequin Mother's Day Contest Winners 2216, P.O. Box 4200 Blair, NE 68009-4200 or you may access the www.eHarlequin.com Web site through June 3, 2002.

Contest sponsored by Torstar Corp., P.O. Box 9042, Buffalo, NY 14269-9042.

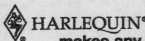